THE
VICTIM
IN
VICTORIA
STATION

JEANNE M. DAMS

D0187558

W☉RLDWIDE.

TORONTO • NEW YORK • LONDON
AMSTERDAM • PARIS • SYDNEY • HAMBURG
STOCKHOLM • ATHENS • TOKYO • MILAN
MADRID • WARSAW • BUDAPEST • AUCKLAND

THE VICTIM IN VICTORIA STATION

A Worldwide Mystery/December 2000

Published by arrangement with Walker Publishing Company, Inc.

ISBN 0-373-26368-6

This one is for Ruth
and Donna, who would
have enjoyed it so.
They were a lot alike;
I hope they've had the
chance to meet,
wherever they are now.

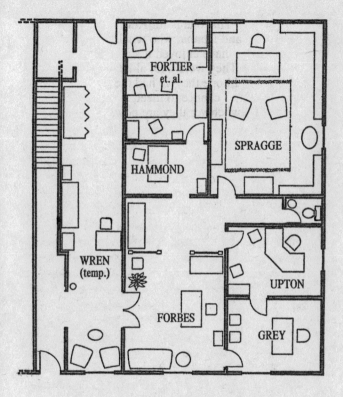

FORTIER
et. al.

SPRAGGE

HAMMOND

WREN
(temp.)

FORBES

UPTON

GREY

MULTILINKS INTL., PLC

ONE

AT LAST! The old, disused Battersea Power Station loomed into view, with its ugly cooling towers that always remind me of dirty milk bottles. Slowing, clicking over the points, we crossed the Thames and slowed further, and then the outside world disappeared from view as the train station enveloped us.

I stood, swaying as the train rocked a little, and gathered my raincoat and umbrella and hat from the rack above. It was a sign of my agitation that I spared little attention for the hat, a frivolous wide-brimmed straw decorated with dozens of little ribbon rosettes. It's one of my favorites, but I was too annoyed just then to be comforted by any hat. Thanks to an infuriating delay near Oxted, I was already nearly an hour late for my doctor's appointment, and I'd be later still by the time I finally reached Harley Street. I could get myself out of the train quickly enough—there was only one other person in the car—but the taxi stand at Victoria Station is a long way from the trains, and I was, by doctor's orders, moving cautiously these days. By the time I made it to the taxis, there'd be a long waiting line.

I stuffed my collapsible umbrella into my purse and glowered at my cane. Drat the thing, anyway! It refused to hook over anything, slithered down into people's way every time I sat down, and made me look like an old woman. Surely I could dispense with it before long? The break in my leg had been somewhat nasty, but it had happened months ago. Oh, the doctor had made long faces and produced irritating comments about the body healing more slowly "at your age," but a pox on that! I *felt* about thirty-five; shouldn't that count for something? This was to be my last appointment with the specialist. I hoped he'd tell me I could now do anything I wanted, especially including running for cabs.

As the train lurched to a stop, I had a sudden thought. The nice young man across the aisle, who was now slumbering peacefully, had offered earlier to share the car that was coming to meet him. I had declined, but perhaps, after all, I'd take him up on it. A friendly person who had admired my hat, he'd seemed perfectly harmless. I hated to wake him, though.

I had gone for a cup of coffee about a half hour before, more for something to do than because I had any great desire for railway coffee, and he'd been asleep when I'd come back from the buffet car. I looked at him now, frowning with indecision. His own coffee cup, fortunately empty, had rolled off the tiny tray table with that last lurch, and his head lolled against the headrest. He looked very uncomfortable. What should I do? I didn't really know him, after all, but he was a fellow American, and we'd chatted pleasantly on the ridiculously protracted journey. He'd said he was still suffering from jet lag after only two days in England, so I could understand his sleepiness, but he was as much overdue for his commitments as I was for mine. I decided it would be a kindness to serve as his alarm clock.

I tapped him on the shoulder. "Ummm…Mr.—" Oh, for heaven's sake, what was his name? Something Irish, I was sure. We'd talked about that. This was his first trip to the U.K., and he was going to look up his Irish forebears if he had time after he finished with his business. Riley, was it? O'Brien? No, something less common than those, but it wasn't coming to me.

His first name I did remember. "Bill! We're here, finally. We're in London. Bill, wake up!" I tapped him again, a little harder.

His head rolled to the side, and his shoulder and torso followed, slumping against me. I suppressed a yelp and tried to move him. He was unresponsive, a deadweight.

Suddenly there didn't seem to be quite enough air in my lungs. I reached with one hand for the handgrip on the back of a seat, and with the other put two fingers under Bill's collar. The flesh was warm, but I could feel no pulse. I gulped and tried to take deep breaths.

"Excuse me, may I pass through?"

I looked back, with infinite relief. Someone had come through from the next car. The man trying to get up the aisle looked, in his darksuit and hat, extremely respectable, a help in time of trouble. "I'm sorry, but this man—well, the fact is, he seems to be…I was just talking to him a little while ago, and it seems impossible, but I think he's—dead."

Why is it so hard to pronounce such a short, simple word?

Mr. Respectable gave me a sharp look. "He must be ill. Let me past, please, I'm a doctor."

Even better! I moved carefully out of the way, trying to keep the pathetic thing that had been Bill from sliding farther out of its seat. I didn't quite like to leave, though I was by this time pretty sure Bill was beyond any help we could provide.

It took Respectable no more than a few seconds to come to the same conclusion. He looked at me blankly. "Is—was he a friend of yours?"

"No, I didn't know him at all, but we talked while the train was stopped. He was a nice man; I can hardly believe—"

"I see." The man looked shaken, though as a doctor he must often have seen death before. Maybe he was a dermatologist, or a chiropodist, or something.

Maybe I'd better stop chasing irrelevancies and think what to do. "I suppose we ought to notify the police," I suggested tentatively, "or will the railway authorities do that? Sudden death, after all."

The doctor sighed and nodded. "Yes, of course. I'll take care of it, though his appearance is quite consistent with heart attack." He shook his head. "A young man. What a pity."

"Isn't it? Is there anything—I mean, I don't quite like to leave, but I'm very late for an appointment...."

"I shouldn't think there's anything for you to do. I have a mobile phone, of course; I'll ring the police and give this poor chap a bit of an examination while

I wait about for them to come. Thank you for your concern, madam, but I believe I can take care of anything further that is required. There's no reason for you to put yourself out."

"Well, then—my name is Martin, Dorothy Martin, and I live in Sherebury, if you should need me for anything."

He thanked me again, with the sort of bored voice that clearly indicated I as becoming a nuisance. The train was empty by this time; I'd be ages getting a taxi. Feeling heartless for leaving the poor man— which was ridiculous—I gathered my things together and walked away.

The streets, when I finally got out into them in one of London's wonderful black cabs, were crowded with traffic. They always are, but today seemed worse than usual. We were fast approaching high tourist season, and that means more foreigners trying to drive on the wrong side of the road. At least it wasn't raining, which creates an even worse snarl, though it looked as though it might start in at any time. A London June at its most typical, in fact.

I usually enjoy the luxury of a cab ride through my favorite city and make the most of it, rubbernecking at familiar landmarks like the rawest tourist, but today I was preoccupied. I spent that ride, and the half hour I had to wait in the doctor's office, thinking about the poor man on the train. He'd been young, as the doctor had remarked, no more than thirty, at a guess. How terrible and unexpected, to have a heart attack at that age! My first husband, Frank, had died of a massive heart attack that had come like a thief in the night to steal him away from me, but he'd been sixty-five and had done a lot of living. Poor Bill had had his life in front of him, or he'd thought he had. He'd never marry that pretty girl now, the one whose picture he carried around with him. He'd never look up those relatives in Ireland. He'd never have the chance to straighten out the problems his company was having in the London office, or even finish the Tom Clancy novel he'd abandoned when we'd started to talk.

He'd never see London. So close, and yet he'd never see one of the world's greatest cities. He'd been looking forward to it, too, after spending the weekend in the country with one of his business associates, recovering from jet lag. His book, *Patriot Games*, began in London, and he was eager to see what he'd been reading about. I twisted in my uncomfortable doctor's-office chair. If I hadn't gone for coffee when I did…if there hadn't been such a long line at the counter…if I'd been more observant, and hadn't just thought he was asleep….

There was no reason why I should feel responsible, but I'd liked young Bill, and he was a fellow American, and I'd wanted to watch his face when he stepped out into glorious London. Maybe I'm a sentimental idiot, but I was near tears by the time the nurse called me in.

At least the doctor, when he had finished examining me and we were seated in his consulting room, had good news for me.

"That's looking splendid, Mrs. Martin," he said, pointing out details of an X ray. "You have the bones of a woman half your age, save for the arthritic joints.

I did not expect a break as bad as this to heal so completely so soon, particularly since you insisted on so much activity. Do you have any pain in the leg now?"

"It aches a little when it rains." Which, in England, was a good percentage of the time, but I decided not to say so. The English can be touchy about their weather.

"Yes, well, that, unfortunately, may persist for quite a time, but on the whole I think I can send you off with a clean bill of health. Do what you want, within reasonable limits, of course. Light housework, shopping, a bit of a walk now and again. Use the cane when you need it. Apart from that"—he shrugged his shoulders—"don't fall down any more stairs!" He laughed.

I was unable to laugh with him. That fall had been one of the most terrifying experiences of my life. If Alan hadn't been there…. "I don't plan to, Dr. Reynolds," I said rather primly.

He composed his face. "No, indeed. I'll give you a prescription for the pain, if you need it, but aspirin ought to provide relief in most cases, or ibuprofen. All right, then?"

I shook his hand and left, rather glad that Dr. Reynolds was not my regular doctor. For most ailments I went to the small clinic in Sherebury, my beloved adopted town. I'd been living in England for almost two years now and had gotten used to the idea of virtually free health care. I'd even established a good relationship with one of the doctors at the clinic. But when I had broken my leg last November, Alan had thought I'd better consult a London orthopedist. I'd murmured something about the exorbitant cost of a private doctor.

"Hang the cost, Dorothy! I've only just got you, woman, and I intend to look after you. Since you insist on getting yourself into trouble, the least I can do is attempt damage control. I'm not a poor man, my dear. And you are very precious to me."

It was the last remark that did it, of course, the words and the tone of voice in which they were uttered. We'd been married only a couple of months then. Alan hadn't uttered a word of anything but sympathy and concern when I'd fallen and broken the leg, even though I had at the time been engaged in dangerous activities of which he didn't entirely approve. I'd felt the least I could do was accept his advice.

It was probably good advice, too, and I had to admit Dr. Reynolds was competent. It was just his attitude that I found a little annoying. He seemed to feel an old lady ought to tend to her knitting.

I don't consider myself old, and I knit very badly.

I'd planned my day so as to avoid the rush hour, but the various delays had plunged me into the very worst of it. Though the Regent's Park tube station wasn't far away, my leg was aching a little, and the Underground would be crowded to suffocation point, so I waited with what patience I could muster and finally managed to snare a cab. My driver was taciturn, unusual in a London cabbie, but I didn't try to make him talk to me. He had plenty to think about, what with the horrendous traffic through which he inched the cab, making some speed in rare clear spaces, then screeching to sudden stops as the stream closed in again.

The *Evening Standard* was being hawked on the street corners; I made a mental note to buy one in the station and see what it said about the man in the train. It was so stupid that I couldn't remember his name.

"Bloody hell!" As the driver swore loudly, the cab stopped with a scream of abused brakes and an ominous crunch. I was nearly thrown off my seat.

"You all right, madam?" He craned his neck around as he was opening his door.

"I think so. What happened?"

"Bleedin' idiot come out o' Buckingham Palace Road there and turned the wrong way, right in front o' me! Naow, then"—this addressed grimly to the other driver—"wot the hell do you think you're doin'?"

We sat there in Lower Grosvenor Place, next to the Royal Mews and the rest of Buckingham Palace's back garden, for quite some time, tying up traffic while my cabbie explained the rules of the road to the other driver. ("I don't bloody care where you're from, you're in England now, and we drive on the *left!*")

Eventually matters were resolved, to the dismay of the other driver, who was dark skinned and spoke with a French accent, and whose rental car had to be towed away. The cab had suffered no worse than a dented fender, but the cabbie was mortally offended. "I own this cab, an' I'll see that bleeder pays! Sorry, madam! It's them foreigners we get everywhere these days, don't know how to talk, don't know how to drive—that'll only be three pounds fifty, madam, never mind the meter, I forgot an' left it runnin' back there. Sorry about the delay, madam—thank you very much!''

I overtipped him out of exhaustion or sympathy and caught a much later train than the one I'd hoped for. By way of small compensation, it was far less crowded than the earlier one would have been, and by miraculous intervention it ran on time. In less than an hour I was at Sherebury station. I stumbled out, climbed into my little Volkswagen, which was looking lonesome in the deserted parking lot, and drove wearily to my house. I just sat for a few minutes in my driveway, very grateful to be home at last.

It would have been even nicer if Alan had been there to greet me, but Alan was out of the country. My husband, Alan Nesbitt (I kept my former name when we married), is a policeman. He had left his position of chief constable for Belleshire several months before to take over temporarily as commandant of the Police Staff College at Bramshill, and we'd had to move to the lovely but, to me, formidable Jacobean manor that housed the college. With that appointment ended, we were able to come back home, but we'd been there barely a month when Alan, now officially retired but still in demand as a consultant all over the world, had to go to Zimbabwe for a conference on terrorism. This was the first time he'd been far away since we were married, and I missed him enormously. Zimbabwe sounds like the end of the earth. Until I looked it up on the map, I didn't even know where it was, exactly, only that it was in Africa and vaguely associated with political problems.

It would have been heaven to have Alan there to talk to. He would have poured us some Jack Daniel's, fixed us something to eat, calmed me down, and listened with interest and sympathy to the saga of how badly my day had gone.

However, only the cats were there to greet me when I finally pried myself out of the car and went into the house, and they displayed little sympathy. They were HUNGRY! Human problems have little importance compared with the urgent needs of cats, who are the ultimate pragmatists.

I pulled off my hat and took some aspirin even before I fed the cats. My head was throbbing almost as much as my leg. By way of food for myself, once my domestic tyrants had been placated, I heated a can of soup and collapsed on the parlor sofa with it and a small jolt of bourbon.

I felt a little better with food and drink inside me and the comfort of my house closing around me. I love my little seventeenth-century cottage. Just sitting in front of the lovely old fireplace, even on a warm evening with no fire, was soothing. Tomorrow, as Scarlett tritely observed, was another day, and I could start planning a more active life now that I was released from medical restrictions. Right now all I wanted to do was sit with a cat on my lap—I reached for Samantha, my Siamese, who was handiest—and read the paper. A little later I'd blow the budget and call Alan. The sound of his voice ought to complete my cure.

But what had I done with the paper? Oh, of course. I smacked my forehead in the classic gesture. I'd forgotten to buy one. The accident in the cab had driven it right out of my head. Drat! I wanted to read about the man in the train, and by morning it might be too late—old news. Alan and I didn't take an evening paper, only the *Times* and the *Telegraph* in the morning. Did Jane, my next-door neighbor, subscribe to the *Standard?* Was I too tired to go over there and find out?

I set Sam aside and stood up. If I let myself give in to "too tired," I'd turn into that decrepit old lady Dr. Reynolds thought I was.

Though it was nearly nine, the sky was still quite light, the long twilight of a northern country in June. I walked across my backyard and tapped on Jane's door. She opened it at once, and she and several of her bulldogs greeted me cordially.

Once we were comfortably seated at her kitchen table, she studied me critically. "Look like something the cat dragged in," she observed. Jane seldom bothers with diplomacy.

"I feel like it, too. It's been a rotten day, Jane. There wouldn't be any coffee, by any chance?"

"Just coming. Kettle's about to boil."

"I've always thought you were psychic."

She snorted. "Saw you coming across the garden. Any fool could see you needed something. There's whiskey if you'd rather."

I shook my head. "I've had as much as is good for me, and anyway I've got a headache. Coffee's better.

Jane, a man died in the train today, on my way to London.''

She raised her eyebrows, but the kettle whistled just then, and she turned to make the coffee. As she poured hot water over the grounds, the bright, modern kitchen was filled with fragrance. (Jane's house is also old, Georgian, but like me she prefers modern convenience when it comes to cooking.) I began to feel invigorated even before she set a cup in front of me and poured out the rich brew from the French press carafe.

"Mostly decaf, this time of the day," Jane announced. "But it tastes real." She let me take a few hot, revivifying sips before she raised her eyebrows again and said, "The man in the train?"

I told her the story. My voice got a little thick in places, and I had to clear my throat and drink some coffee.

"Upsetting," said Jane with masterly British understatement. "Who was he?"

"I can't remember! You know I'm never especially good about names. Bill something. That's one reason I came over. I wanted to look at your *Standard,* if you have one."

"Help yourself. Nothing in it about a dead man in a train, not that I noticed."

She handed me the paper. I skimmed quickly, frowned, and looked again more carefully. "No, nothing," I said finally, disappointed. "Maybe it happened after their deadline. I'll have to check in the morning."

"Why?"

I sighed. "I don't know, really. I guess I feel involved. I didn't even know him, but I liked him. I need to know what happened, who he was. I—it sounds silly, but I think I want to mourn him properly."

Jane gave me a long look, and when she spoke it was gruffly. "Not thinking there was something funny about the death, are you?"

"Jane! I admit that I've been somewhat more involved in murder than most respectable women, but I plead not guilty this time. No, this is pure curiosity, with some sorrow mixed in. I simply want to know what happened, so I can stop feeling there was something I might have been able to do."

"Glad to hear it."

When I got home, I decided my spirits had improved enough that I didn't need to call Alan. It was really too late, anyway; he was a couple of time zones away. Tomorrow would do, when I'd read the paper and could give him a coherent account. For now, the miserable day had finally dragged itself to a close, and I'd never have to live that particular one again. And tomorrow would be a good day to make a nice cozy phone call; it was certainly going to rain, if my leg was any sort of weather prophet at all. Followed eagerly by the cats, I went upstairs, took a couple of pain pills, and fell into welcome sleep almost as soon as the three of us were comfortably arranged on the bed.

TWO

IT WAS THE CATS who woke me. Esmeralda ran her claws into my thigh, and I jerked into semiconsciousness, glancing at the clock. It was a little after three.

"Emmy! Bad cat! What did you do that for—?" I stopped because I could see, in the dim glow of the night-light in the hall, that Sam's slender tail was bushed out like a bottlebrush, and her ears, fully alert, were turned toward the hall door. Somewhere, probably next door, dogs were barking hysterically.

I caught my breath and heard Emmy give a low growl. In the same moment I heard glass breaking, and both cats jumped off the bed and raced downstairs.

I didn't think twice. The phone was right next to the bed. I picked it up, punched in the emergency number with fingers that trembled, and whispered to the responder, "Someone is trying to break into my house."

The four minutes that it took them to get there seemed like hours. I waited until I heard the reassuring voices of several policemen before venturing out of bed, and then I thought I'd never get my bathrobe on, my hands were shaking so.

"Mrs. Martin!" The voice that called up the stairs wasn't familiar, but it was welcome. "I'm Sergeant Drew. Are you all right?"

"I'm fine," I lied. "I'm coming down."

"Don't forget to put on slippers. There's a good deal of broken glass in the kitchen."

The next hour or so was a jumble of confusion. The house seemed full of people and animals. There were two policemen and one policewoman, and my cats, and Jane, and one of her bulldogs. "Brought him along just in case," she explained gruffly. "Didn't know what was happening over here, glass breaking. Damn fool thing for me to do. Scaring the cats into fits."

That wasn't quite true; the cats were furious rather than frightened. It was the dog that whined and rolled his eyes and tugged at his leash. Emmy had clawed his nose once, and dogs have long memories. Eventually Jane, reassured that I was unhurt, took him home, and I was left with the police.

They searched the house thoroughly, inside and out, but found no one. That endless four minutes had apparently been long enough for the burglar to get away. "The chap was pretty thorough," said Sergeant Drew. "Tried all the ground-floor windows before he broke the glass in the back door. A good job you had the new locks put in. He couldn't unlock it even from inside without the key."

"It's also a good thing Alan thought to give a key to you people, or *you* wouldn't have been able to get in, and I'd probably have stepped in all that glass. And it's just pure luck that the downstairs windows were closed. I thought it was going to rain, and I didn't want to have to mop up puddles in the morning. I do appreciate your getting here so fast. I was in a real panic.''

"We look after our own, Mrs. Martin. We were all sorry when the chief retired. He's a good man.''

"He certainly is.'' I found I had to swallow a couple of times, hard. "What do we do now?''

"You'd best go back to bed. We'll see to cleaning up the glass. Because of the possibility of fingerprints or other evidence,'' he added, seeing the query on my face. "We'll also look after boarding up the door, and we'll leave WPC Murray here to look after you.''

"Oh, I don't think that's necessary,'' I said weakly. Woman Police Constable Murray, who was standing by Sergeant Drew, looked like the epitome of sanity and comfort, and in fact her presence would be very welcome. I was still shaking.

"It's standard procedure when a police family is threatened, Mrs. Martin. This was probably just a standard break-and-enter robbery attempt, but one can never be certain.''

"I can't imagine why anyone would think we had anything to steal, but you must be right. Unless—I suppose Alan must have made some enemies in all those years on the force. Has anyone gotten out of jail lately who hated him particularly?''

Sergeant Drew grinned. "Not likely, I shouldn't think. The wide boys usually blame the copper who collars them, or the judge, or even the jury. They don't know the chief constable exists. No, it'll be someone who thought this looked a nice house, worth a go. He'll be long gone, of course, but we'll keep an eye out.''

"Well then, I confess I'll be very glad of Constable Murray's company, if you're sure you can spare her. I get rather nervous when Alan's away."

"Yes, of course. Now, do you have Mr. Nesbitt's telephone number where he's staying? We can find out, of course, if you don't have it handy—"

"Oh, I have it, but do you have to notify him? I'd rather he didn't know until I get a chance to tell him myself. I'm afraid he would worry, and he's doing such important work, I—I don't like to distract him."

Sergeant Drew nodded soothingly. "Of course," he said again. "I thought you might want him to know first thing in the morning, but as you wish. You do look tired, if you'll excuse my saying so. Miss Murray, can you see Mrs. Martin to bed?"

I felt, and probably looked, like death warmed over. I gratefully accepted WPC Murray's assistance up the stairs, told her to help herself to coffee or anything else she wanted, and fell into bed. This time my sleep was undisturbed, except by dreams.

It was shamefully late by the time I finally made myself get up the next morning. True, I had all kinds of excuses, and there was nothing in particular I had to do that day, but I've never been able to shake the notion that sleeping late is somehow discreditable. Too many years spent living up to the work ethic, I suppose. At any rate, I sent WPC Murray on her way, after making sure that she had indeed made herself some breakfast.

"Are you quite sure you'll not feel nervous alone?"

"Quite sure. I'm rested, and it's daylight, and I'd

feel really guilty if I took up the time of a hardworking policewoman when you're so understaffed. Off you go!''

"Daylight" was something of a euphemism. It was one of the darkest summer days I'd ever known. True to my tibia's forecast, the rain was coming down in torrents, and the sky was dark blue-gray. I would actually have liked to have a bite to eat and then go back to bed, but I was stern with myself. Old ladies do that sort of thing. Active middle-aged women face the day with alacrity.

You've got to be kidding, said an inner voice.

Well, if alacrity wasn't in the cards, I'd try to muster something more positive than sleepy gloom, anyway. I made fresh coffee, very strong, and after a couple of cups had pumped some life into my system, I sat down with the papers. Half an hour later there was enough adrenaline in my system to make the caffeine redundant.

There was no mention of my dead man in either paper.

I hadn't expected headlines, but surely a dead American, found in rather unusual circumstances, was worth a small paragraph! I felt insulted, personally and patriotically. Okay, London is a big city, and people die there every day, but not foreigners, not in a train, not of a heart attack at age thirty or so. How could they just ignore it?

Would CONNEX, the railway company, be any help? It seemed unlikely. Since the demise of British Rail and the privatization of what used to be England's admirable rail system, I've almost never found any railway official to be of the slightest help about anything. It was, however, worth a try.

Several phone calls later, my opinion of the railway bureaucracy was left unchanged. Nobody knew of a dead man in any train that had called at Victoria Station. Nobody thought it at all likely that such a thing had occurred. Nobody considered that anyone, much less an American, would have the temerity to die in any train operated by CONNEX. Thank you, madam.

Very well. I hadn't wanted to bother the police. It was, in any case, highly unlikely that the Metropolitan Police would release to me the name of the young man. However, there was no point in being married to a very important, if retired, policeman if one didn't use the connection now and again.

I picked the phone back up and put in a call to Detective Chief Inspector Morrison, the most senior police officer I knew. He called back in five minutes.

"This is a pleasure, Mrs. Martin. Not found another body for us, have you?"

The Inspector and I had first met over a body in the town hall.

"Not really," I said with a rueful laugh. "This time it's more a case of my wanting you to find one for me."

"Yes? An unusual taste, if you'll forgive my saying so. But to each her own."

"Maybe I phrased that badly. Let me explain."

I did so, detailing the circumstances, the day and time the train got to Victoria, and a description of the dead man for good measure.

"I do understand that it's really none of my concern, but I'd feel a lot better if I knew who the man was and how he died. I keep thinking there ought to have been something I could do. I know you're busy, but I didn't think Scotland Yard would listen to me.''

"You might be surprised," he replied, rather cryptically, I thought. "But I can speed things up. I've rather a lot on my plate, as usual, but I'll make a few inquiries and report back.''

I puttered around the kitchen, cleaning up bits of glass that the police had missed. I should call someone to replace the window in the back door. The piece of wood that covered the gaping hole was not only unsightly, it darkened both the kitchen and my spirits. I'd never had my house broken into before, and the shattered window was a disquieting reminder. Last night I'd been afraid of the intruder. This morning, I was pleased to discover, I was angry, a much more useful emotion. My house had been invaded, or nearly invaded, and damaged in the process. I had been terrified. How dare someone do that! How DARE they!

The last straw was the tiny overlooked shard of glass that had somehow flown across the room to the kitchen counter, where I managed to run it into the pad of my thumb as I tidied up. That did it. For five minutes I was simply, gloriously furious, indulging in language I hadn't known I knew.

Pounding my fist on the counter, however, was the final gesture of my tantrum. It jarred the sliver of glass in my thumb, which hurt—a lot. The pain jolted me back to my senses. I looked around a little guiltily for the cats. They had fled when the storm broke. My wrath hadn't seemed to be directed at them, but a cat can't be too careful. I had the fleeting, foolish thought that I was glad they didn't understand enough human speech to know what I'd been saying. Then I went up to the bathroom to find the tweezers.

I'd managed to pry the sliver out of my thumb when the phone rang. I picked it up in the bedroom. It was Inspector Morrison's secretary.

"The chief inspector asked me to say he's sorry he couldn't ring you back himself, Mrs. Martin. He's been called away to an incident." Which could mean anything up to murder. "However, he was able to talk to the Metropolitan Police. They state that no bodies were found in trains coming into London yesterday, nor for months. They checked all stations for good measure. There were no such reports. In fact, it was a quiet day at the stations; the police were called to two pickpocket incidents and one stolen luggage. That was the extent of it."

"But that can't be true! I saw the man myself! And the doctor told me he was going to report it to the police right away."

"Perhaps the man was only comatose, Mrs. Martin. To the layman—"

"But the doctor wasn't a layman, and he quite definitely said the man was dead!"

A silence fell, a silence that became, imperceptibly, quite heavily tactful.

"I see," said the secretary finally. "Quite a mystery. When Inspector Morrison returns—"

I pulled myself together. "No, don't bother. He's busy. I expect I made some sort of mistake. Thank him for me."

I hung up before I lost my temper. On the whole, I thought it was a good thing I'd expended all that emotional energy on the sliver of glass and my intruder. I was left with less to waste on an impervious Scotland Yard.

Mistake! Of course I hadn't made a mistake. That man had been dead as—as a coffin nail, Dickens would have said. So why didn't the police know about him?

Because they weren't notified, said the other half of my brain calmly.

But the doctor said—

What doctor? Do you believe everything you're told?

My temper deflated rapidly. I had, hadn't I? Oh, my, how naive of me. At my age, and with my somewhat unusual background, one would have thought I'd be more critical. The respectable-looking man had called himself a doctor. I'd believed him. He had said he was going to call the police. I'd believed that, too.

He'd also said the dead man was the victim of a heart attack. That, I was beginning not to believe at all.

I went slowly downstairs, picked up the telephone pad, and sat down at the kitchen table. What did I know about the dead man? I started to make a list.

I knew his first name.

Bill? went down on the list.

American.

First time in England.

Here on business.

Here I paused. What kind of business? He'd told

me, I was sure. It's one of the standard set of questions strangers ask each other—where are you from, what do you do, are you married, do you have children, et cetera. He was from California. I remembered that, because I have family there. And he worked in—

Of course! He worked in Silicon Valley somewhere, and he worked with computers! My memory grudgingly released details, a few at a time. Bill's concern was, specifically, computer software. He was a partner in a small but growing company. That much I had understood. He had told me in great detail exactly what his company's software did, and why it was so wonderful, and how the tiny two-man operation had grown so rapidly into an international concern. That part hadn't made sense to me even at the time, so of course I couldn't remember much. I know very little about computers, which fascinate and scare me at the same time. I did remember, though, that he had told me he'd come to England to look into problems in the London office. Had he used the phrase "growing pains," or was that simply the impression I'd gained from what he did say?

I sat back, rather pleased with myself. I not only had a few facts in front of me, dredged up from my uncooperative mind, but I had an idea. Its name was Nigel Evans.

Nigel Evans was a graduate student at Sherebury University and a good friend of mine. I'd met him my first Christmas in Sherebury, when I'd been instrumental in saving him from something pretty unpleasant. He'd often said he wished he could do something for me. Well, now was his chance.

For Nigel, at age twenty-something, was a shark at computers. He was doing research in history, but he also worked part-time in the university's Computer Centre. He had at one time told me exactly what he did there, but of course the jargon had gone in one ear and out the other. I did know, because his delightful young wife, Inga, had told me, that Nigel subscribed to virtually every computer magazine known to man, and knew more about what Bill Gates and Steve Jobs were doing than he did about their neighbors. Inga, greatly to her amusement, had had to explain who Gates and Jobs were.

Nigel was my source of information. And Nigel was the son-in-law of my favorite pubkeepers, the Endicotts at the Rose and Crown, just on the other side of the cathedral. I looked at the kitchen clock. Nearly noon, and I'd had no breakfast. All right, there was no time like the present. I picked up my umbrella and my purse, plucked a rainproof hat off one of the pegs in the hallway, and headed for the gate at the end of my street that led into the Cathedral Close.

THREE

Despite the rain, I dillydallied a bit on the walk to the cathedral, through it, and out again to the Rose and Crown. My leg ached enough that a slow pace seemed wiser, especially over rain-slick paving stones, but then I always like to take my time in and around the cathedral. I still have to pinch myself now and then to make sure I'm not dreaming, that I really do live next door to all that age and beauty and magnificence. I never want to get used to it, take it for granted.

It wasn't a good day for pausing outside to look up at the buttresses and pinnacles, but once I was inside the church, I followed my usual practice of wandering idly for a few minutes, trying to find some lovely detail I hadn't noticed before. Today a small stained glass window in the south aisle caught my eye, and I was puzzling over it when the Dean's wife appeared at my elbow.

"He's very gorgeous, our Satan, isn't he?" she said.

"Almost too gorgeous," I said, looking at the feathers of purple and scarlet and gold that were flying from the deposed angel's wings as he fell headlong from heaven. "He actually looks very attractive, if it weren't for those eyes."

"Oh, but Satan *is* attractive! Proud and bold and

beautiful—the angel of the morning, you know. Evil always has to be gaudier and more glamorous than good, or it wouldn't draw any converts at all.'' She looked at the window thoughtfully. ''The windows were their Sunday schools then, of course. They didn't have Bibles—the parishioners, I mean—and most people couldn't have read them even if they'd had them. So the church decorations were meant to teach them the stories.''

''This one is a terrible story,'' I said soberly. ''And rather a horrible picture, if you look at it closely.''

''Yes, and rightly so. It took Milton to turn the devil into a hero, and that wasn't for another couple of hundred years after this window was made. The Middle Ages understood the price of pride, Dorothy. Look at what Satan's leaving behind, so that he can rule, rather than serve. And you mentioned his eyes. Of course they're frightening. They're looking down into hell. Into death.'' She paused. ''My dear, what is it? What have I said?''

She had seen my face change. ''Nothing, really. Just your mention of looking into death. I had a bad experience yesterday.'' I turned deliberately away from the disturbing window and told her the story, or an abbreviated version. I was beginning to be very worried indeed about Bill's death. I'd dismissed Jane's suggestion of murder lightly enough last night, but that was before the dearth of information in the papers had made me think the whole thing had been hushed up. Maybe I was falling prey to senile paranoia, but I wasn't sure I wanted to tell very many people about the dead man I was beginning to think of as "mine." Margaret, of course, was perfectly discreet, but still....

"O, dear. How awful for you! Though for him, of course—"

I nodded. "A nice clean instant death. But to be murdered—"

"I doubt that matters to him very much now," said Margaret matter-of-factly. "I'll ask Kenneth to pray for him. Bill, you said?"

"It's all I can remember."

"Never mind. God knows his name. I must go, my dear. Are you quite sure you're all right?"

"I'm fine. I was just going to the Rose and Crown for some lunch."

"Let me see—Wednesday. Cottage pie. Enjoy it, and don't worry too much."

She bustled off, and I breathed a small sigh. In this place of peace and goodwill, this temporal place so closely linked to the eternal, the sudden death of a young man disappeared with barely a ripple. Perhaps in the vast cosmic scheme of things, that was appropriate, but I wasn't able to accept death as easily as Margaret could. I still wanted some answers.

I headed for the west door.

"Hul-lo, my love!" boomed Peter Endicott as I entered the lovely old inn. "Haven't seen you in donkey's years. Where've you been keeping yourself?" Mine host, looking the part right down to the rosy cheeks and spotless white apron, offered me his arm and showed me to a table in the raftered, paneled bar. I was the only customer; noon is a little early for lunch in England. "What'll it be, then?"

"Margaret Allenby said this is cottage pie day."

"It is that, and very nice today, too. You'd like a pint of bitter with it, would you, or a glass of claret?"

"Bitter, please, but just a half." I relaxed into the Governor Winthrop chair, so much more comfortable than it looked, and drank in my surroundings. The Rose and Crown is, to me, exactly what a pub ought to be. It's a warm place, in both senses, partly because of Peter's genial personality and partly because of the beautiful old wood and the low ceiling and the diamond-paned windows and the brass ornaments hung here and there. The Endicotts refuse to succumb to the enticements of canned music or the electronic game machines that turn so many other pubs into a hideous clangor of noise. They draw their customers by encouraging conversation and serving excellent bar food, at reasonable prices, during the day, and four-star meals at night in the elegant dining room on the other side of the entry hall. Upstairs a few tastefully decorated rooms provide luxurious lodging for lucky travelers. They always come back.

"Dorothy, you're looking blooming!" said Peter as he drew my beer and dished up my lunch from the small steam table behind the bar. "But you really haven't been round for ages, have you now?"

"Well, we only got back from Bramshill last month, and then Alan had to go chasing off to Zimbabwe, a conference he'd promised months ago to attend. He'll be gone for another week or two at least, I imagine. I miss him. Oh, thank you, that looks delicious." I took a bite of the concoction of meat and vegetables and mashed potatoes, spluttered, and downed a quick swallow of beer. "Ouch, hot! Actually, Alan being gone is one reason I stopped in, in a way."

I had already decided to be less than candid with Peter. He was a good friend, an old friend, but he talked to a lot of people in the course of a day, many of them strangers, and I couldn't rid myself of that nasty feeling that too much talk about my train victim might prove unwise. "You see," I went on, hoping I sounded honest, "Alan thinks it might be a good idea for me to get a computer, to keep me amused whenever he's gone. He's officially retired, of course, but he knows too much about too many aspects of policing for people to let him get by with much frittering. So he'll be traveling often, and he worries about me. I could learn a lot from the Internet and the Web, he says, and do some shopping from my own living room, and even keep in touch with people—that sort of thing." I crossed my fingers. Was I explaining too elaborately? Was I using at least some of the right words? "And of course I don't know a thing about it, so I was hoping Nigel might—"

"Of course! The very person! He can tell you everything you want to know, and probably a lot you don't, as well. H's a fine lad, mind, but he does love the sound of his own voice. The Welsh streak, I reckon." Peter laughed comfortably.

"I'm glad to hear the recommendation," I said. I was, too. There had been a time when Peter hadn't liked Nigel too well, and had been very much opposed to his relationship with Inga, Peter's adored daughter. It sounded as though he had been won over completely. Which was a relief, especially as I had been instrumental, in a small way, in bringing about their marriage.

My lunch cooled to an acceptable level, and I ate quite a bit more of it before I ventured the question. "Where can I find Nigel today, Peter? I'm eager to get started on this project, now that Alan's talked me into it."

"Oh, dear, I don't keep his schedule in my head, but Greta would know, I imagine. She's upstairs. I'll just go and fetch her."

"Oh, not if she's busy, Peter. I can easily phone later—"

"No, she'll be coming down in half a mo' anyway, to help with the lunch crowd. They'll be here shortly. Darling!" he called as he went out into the hall and started up the stairs.

Peter's wife, when she came down, was as lovely as ever, which is saying a good deal. She was dressed with her usual simplicity in a black skirt and a white blouse with simple pearl stud earrings, and as usual I thought that the pearls weren't really necessary. When you have a perfect oval face, apple-blossom skin, and the kind of blue eyes poets write sonnets about, you don't need further ornament. Greta was probably in her late forties, but her only sign of age was a silver streak in her golden hair, and even that looked as though she'd had it done in a salon.

She came over and touched her satin cheek to mine. "I couldn't believe it when Peter told me you were here! You've stayed away far too long."

"I have. You're right. I should keep my friendships

in better repair. That's one reason I'm so glad Alan
and I are back in town. Or at least, I am. Alan's
away—did Peter tell you?—and I'm finding myself
at loose ends. That's why I want to see Nigel.'' I
repeated the elaborate fiction I'd told Peter. ''Would
he have time today to give me a few pointers on how
to pick out a computer?''

''Today, let's see. Wednesday. He has classes all
morning on Wednesdays, I know, but I believe he
works at the Computer Centre all afternoon.''

''Oh, then he won't be free until this evening?'' I
tried not to let my disappointment show. If my story
were true and it really were just a case of seeking his
advice, it wouldn't be all that urgent.

Greta laughed, the silvery laugh that was so like
her daughter's. ''My dear! So far as I can understand
it, Nigel's work consists entirely of messing about on
the Internet, unless one of the students needs his help
with a project, and this close to the end of term that
isn't likely. They're finishing their projects, not
launching them, and they've no time for computer
nonsense, games and that sort of thing. I should think
he'd have hours to chat with you.''

''Good! Now, just where do I find the Computer
Centre?''

It was, fortunately, on the edge of the campus.
Sherebury University is built on the hills to the northwest of the town proper, and though I often enjoy
walking its spacious, beautiful, American-style campus, I didn't want to do it in the rain with an aching
leg. I went home and got the VW out of the garage,
carefully negotiated the short trip to the university,

and was lucky enough to find a space in a visitors' parking lot quite close to the little building that housed the computers.

A kind student in the front hall showed me where to find Nigel. "Just through there, madam, and then the third door on your left. You won't have any trouble finding him." He glanced at my gray hair, noted my limp, and tried to hide his smile. A polite young man.

"You're never too old to learn, are you?" I said brightly. Shaking out my umbrella, I hobbled off in the direction he had indicated.

I did not, in fact, have any trouble finding Nigel. He was the only person in the room. Either end-of-term studies or the rain had apparently discouraged all the other students. Nigel, intent on his work, didn't look up as I entered, so I took a moment to study him.

Nigel is certainly worth looking at. His coloring is striking—very dark hair, very light skin, deep blue eyes with long lashes. When I first met him he was far too thin, but a year or so of Inga's tender loving care had changed thin to slim and muscular. He can, when he wants to, exercise enormous charm, which almost always gets him what he's after. He can also flare up in a hasty temper, which was why I stood there trying to assess his mood. His frown looked more like one of concentration than anger. I hoped so; I wanted his cooperation to be willing.

His concentration was so deep, in fact, that I had a little trouble attracting his attention. His eyes were fixed on the screen in front of him as his right hand moved a mouse and occasionally clicked a button.

I sat down next to him. "Nigel."

"Ummm. Just one minute, I've almost—"

"Nigel, look at me."

He looked up. I was gratified to see the quick annoyance change to sheer, blazing surprise. "Mrs. Martin. What on earth brought you here?"

Never has anyone had a better cue. "Officially, for the record, I'm here to get your advice on purchasing a home computer. Actually," I said, loading my voice with all the drama I could muster, "I came hoping you could help me unmask a murderer."

FOUR

His STARE, at least for a moment, was all I could have hoped for. His mouth really did drop open, his gorgeous blue eyes did bulge. Then he spoiled it all by breaking out into a roar of laughter.

"You should go on the stage, Mrs. Martin. I actually believed you for a moment."

"You rate my talents too highly. I meant it, Nigel."

His laughter died. "You—you're not serious!"

"I am, indeed. Or at least I think there's a distinct possibility something nasty is afoot. Don't look so skeptical, young man! You, of all people, have reason to know I do occasionally unmask murderers."

For Nigel had been personally involved in a tragedy involving several deaths during my first eventful year in Shrewbury.

"Well—yes. But—"

"But nothing Nigel, can anyone hear us?"

He looked at me closely. "Good Lord, you are serious! No, I don't think we can be heard. This is an old building. The walls on either side are pretty thick, and the door fits well. Unless someone comes in to work at the computers, we're absolutely private."

"And none of these machines can...can—"

"Spy on us?" He didn't laugh. "No. I've made sure."

It was my turn to stare. "I think I only meant, can they hear us? And I was joking, or almost. Do you mean to say they actually *can* spy?"

"Computers can be wired to transmit both audio and video images to another computer. It's a highly specialized application, but there are students here who would know the technology. I do, for one. That's how I know these ones are all right. You can tell me—whatever it is you have to tell me."

He still sounded dubious.

"At this stage it's more a matter of asking you, and I'm going to sound very confused, I expect. But I'm beginning to think I've stumbled into something very odd. Can you keep this quiet, what we're about to talk about?"

"Depends what it is. I tell everything to Inga."

Ah, young love! "That's very commendable of you, and the way it should be, but I don't want it to go any further. Agreed?"

He shrugged and spread his hands, a little amused. "All right."

"Okay, I know I sound like James Bond, but— well, you'll see. Now, what I need first from you, Nigel, is a name. You see, I think I met a murderer yesterday, but I don't know who he is, or even who the victim is."

I told him the story of my dead man and the "doctor," omitting nothing. I told him about my futile search for information in the papers and from the railway.

"Yes, but that doesn't mean anything. It wasn't a very spectacular story, after all, a man dying from a heart attack. It happens every day. And rail personnel in the U.K. have a fixed policy of being unhelpful. You ought to have lived here long enough to know that.''

"All right, how about the police? I got in touch with Scotland Yard through the police here in Shere-bury, and they said they knew nothing about it, either. No dead man. Period.''

Nigel frowned. "That's odd, I admit, but there must be some explanation. Maybe you—''

"Nigel Evans, if you say I imagined the whole thing, I'll throw something right through that computer screen! The man was dead. I've seen enough dead people to know. And as I said at the beginning, I need you to tell me who he was.''

"Right.'' Nigel didn't believe me, and he was getting bored. I hurried on. "I can remember a little; I worked it out this morning. His first name is Bill; I told you that. I remembered because I have a nephew named Bill, and they look a little alike. And he's of Irish descent—the dead man, I mean. That's probably where he got his looks.''

Nigel, who is half Welsh and despises the Irish, snorted.

"It's not much to go on, I know. But he was one of the partners in a software company that's apparently going great guns.'' I told him the few things I'd remembered. Faint indications of interest were beginning to stir, I could see.

"Do you remember anything at all about the sort of software he was involved with?'' he asked after a moment.

"Nothing. It didn't mean anything to me."

"But was it application software, or an operating system, or a specialized database, or some kind of browser, or—"

"Nigel, stop! All those words are—just *words* to me."

He sighed elaborately and ran a hand through his thick black hair. "Right, got you. We start at square one. Have you ever heard of word processing?"

"Of course. Writers use it. Kind of like typing, only on a computer."

Nigel rolled his eyes skyward, but nodded. "Okay. Sort of. How about spreadsheets?"

I shook my head.

"If a word processor is sort of like a very smart typewriter, then a spreadsheet is like a combination of a ledger and a calculator. It's used for bookkeeping." Nigel's voice took on a kind tone, that of the patient teacher explaining to the five-year-old why one plus one equals two. "I'll make it easy. Suppose that you want to balance your checkbook. First you must make certain you've entered all the figures correctly, then you must do all the sums, to be sure your records match up with the statement from the bank. If you kept your checkbook on a computer spreadsheet, it would do all that automatically. So long as all your entries were made properly, you couldn't make a mistake."

"I see," I said with little enthusiasm. In nearly fifty years of writing checks, I've had trouble reconciling my record with the bank statement twice. Both times it was the mistake of the bank.

"Well, then, take another example. I know, your recipe file. You probably use one of those pretty little boxes with cards in it."

I nodded, but my brows knit in a puzzled frown.

"Every time you want to find a recipe, you have to go through the file and try to remember whether you filed that one under meat or entrée, pudding or gateau, right?"

I smiled at that. "How do you know about recipe files?"

"Greta has one. She's a brilliant cook, my mum-in-law, but it takes her ages to find a recipe."

"Well, actually, mine's probably even worse than hers, because I cut things out of magazines and then forget to file them at all, so I'll be looking for a recipe that uses up the roast beef I have left over, and end up two days later finding it under a pile of crossword puzzles."

"Aha! Now, there you have a perfect use for a database program. You type those recipes into your computer, and then later when you want to use up roast beef, you just type in 'beef' and hit the search key, and it finds all the beef recipes. Or it'll keep an address book for you, one that can't get lost or have the pages fall out. Or a Christmas card list."

"All right, I begin to see. Actually I think Meg was using something like that—oh, nobody you know, just someone I met out at the Museum of Miniatures last year. But she was going through an awful lot of work to get all the information typed in."

"Yes, well, entering data is a pain; I'll give you that. But the point is, these are all common uses for a computer that the average person can apply to ordinary life. That's one reason these programs are called application software.''

The light dawned. "Oh, Nigel, that's very good. I do begin to understand. But we haven't gotten any further, because I don't think what Bill talked about was any of those things."

"I didn't think so, either," said Nigel cheerfully, "because all that stuff has been around for years, and there's nothing fabulous and new on the horizon in that area, not really. But there are lots more possibilities. Now, did he at any time use the word 'windows'?''

"Windows? The windows on the train didn't open, if that's what you mean. It was air-conditioned. But why would he be talking about windows when we were discussing computers?''

This time Nigel's laughter lasted till he had tears in his eyes. "I—I'm sorry, Mrs. Martin," he said shakily when he could speak again. "That was beastly rude of me. But really—have you ever heard of Bill Gates?''

"Of course," I said with lofty dignity. "He makes computers, or something, and he's richer than the Queen." I didn't mention how I had come by that information, or how recently.

"Richer than God, is the usual comparison. But he doesn't make computers, he makes software, or his company does. And his best-known product is an operating system, or a series of operating systems— that's the basic software that makes a computer know how to do everything else—called Windows. I can absolutely guarantee that nobody who comes up with any other operating system is going to talk about it without comparing it to Windows. So if *your* Bill didn't say the word, he wasn't talking about a new operating system. We progress."

"If only by elimination."

"Exactly. Can you remember if he talked about the Internet, or the Web?"

"Yes!" I was triumphant. "Yes, he did! I remember now. That was what it was! Nigel, you're wonderful. He said it was a—a motor, I think he said, does that make sense? To use on the Internet. And he said it made things much easier for people doing business in other countries, because—I can't remember why...." I trailed off doubtfully.

Nigel's boredom had evaporated completely. His voice dropped in pitch and began to hum with excitement. "A search engine, was that it?"

"Yes! Engine, not motor, that's right."

"And it incorporates a universal interpreter to search in other languages?"

I was struck with awe. "Nigel, I think that's it! How did you know?"

He had to swallow before he could answer. "Because, if you're talking about what I think you are, it's the hottest piece of software on the market, at least for business use. And, Mrs. Martin, if your story is true, this is going to be very big news all over the world. I think you're telling me Bill Monahan's dead."

"Monahan! Yes!" I was filled with the almost physical relief that comes when we finally pin down something we've been trying to remember. "I knew you were the person to come to. You're a genius."

"Mrs. Martin," Nigel said intently, "it doesn't take a genius to know you could be in serious trouble. If someone's murdered Bill Monahan—good lord, *Monahan*—and they think you can identify them—" He whistled softly.

"But why is he so important? You make him sound like a cross between a prime minister and a rock star. I've never heard of him."

"A few years ago nobody had ever heard of Bill Gates, either."

"Are you saying—?"

"Look, I think I need to explain a little about the computer industry." He leaned back in his chair and stretched his cramped fingers. "Computers have been around for a good deal longer than people realize, but back in the early days they were monsters. Have you ever heard of Univac?"

"Yes, of course, dear. I'm surprised you have." I felt I had to get a little of my own back. "Most of you children know nothing of what happened before you were born."

He ignored my attempt at patronizing. "Did you ever see Univac?"

I shook my head.

"Neither did I, naturally, but I've seen pictures. It occupied the whole of a large room. It required special air-conditioning. It took centuries to complete a task, by today's standards, and it had far less power and capacity than the most rudimentary of today's laptops. It was of use only to businesses and research scientists. And that was the way computers were for the first couple of decades.

"The chaps who started to change things were Bill Gates, on the one hand, and Steve Jobs and Steve Wozniak, on the other. They were your basic nerds, working out of their garages, but what they developed, working independently, was what led to these machines in here." He gestured to the room full of computers.

"The Jobs-Wozniak version eventually became Apple, computers sold complete with all the programs installed. Gates concentrated on ways to make computers more useful to ordinary people, what we now call software, and his company eventually became Microsoft. These three blokes, working with nothing, essentially, except brilliant minds, became the industry leaders, worldwide. They changed the world forever. Bill Monahan is—or was, if we're right—the same sort of chap. That's the way the computer industry is, you see. One person—or two; Bill's partner is Walter Shepherd—can begin with nothing and become a multimillionaire almost overnight. Monahan's company, Multilinks International, was on its way to the top. Now—who knows?" Nigel shrugged elaborately, and I sat there, stunned.

What in the world had I gotten into?

"Good heavens," I said finally.

"Right."

I pulled myself together. "Well, but Nigel—I still don't understand. It sounds as though these early men did lots of things, really advanced, totally new things.

Why should one thing, one piece of software, make such a difference now to one small company?''

''Because that's the way life is nowadays. Gates and Jobs and Wozniak were pioneers. They invented the wheel. Now anyone who figures out a radically new way to make it spin can be rich by tomorrow— if not on his own, then through being bought out by the big guns. And Monahan and his friends came up with an incredible spin.''

I sighed. ''Explain it to me. In words of one syllable.''

Nigel sighed in turn. ''It's not easy to explain to someone who knows nothing about the Internet, but I'll try. Or no, I'll show you. Look.''

He moved the mouse, and the swirling pattern that had filled his screen disappeared. Peering through the bottom of my bifocals, I saw a screen full of lists and boxes.

''What would you like to know about?'' Nigel asked with a grin. ''Anything. Cabbages to kings.''

I was willing to play the game, if it eventually brought him around to the point. ''Um. Kings.''

''Any one in particular?''

''Henry the Eighth.''

Nigel tapped out ''King Henry VIII'' on the keyboard; it appeared in one of the boxes. He clicked his mouse. A moment or two went by with nothing happening, and then the screen changed. Nigel pointed.

''You see that number? The computer found that many references to the old devil.''

I read the number in disbelief. ''Does that really say over a million? How could that be? And what good is it? It would take months to sort through all that material.''

Nigel gave a satisfied little nod. ''Exactly. The problem is the search engine—the program that just went through all the databases it uses. Because of the way this particular search engine is configured, it looked for the words 'king' and 'Henry' and the numeral 'VIII,' and has listed every single source for even one of those referents.''

''But that's foolish. I could do much better going to an encyclopedia.''

''You're quite right. Now, there are ways I could limit the search and get better results, closer to what we want. Or there are other search engines I could use. In fact, I'll do that.''

He moved the mouse around. An arrow on the screen also moved, pointing to various locations. Nigel clicked here and clicked there and typed in something else, and eventually a new list appeared.

''2,427,'' I read. ''That's still a lot, but it's much more manageable.''

''And they're much more to the point.'' Nigel clicked the mouse again, and the screen began to move, rolling up like movie credits. ''Look at the references. An encyclopedia, a history book, another encyclopedia—and if you'll look at the précis with each entry you'll see they all refer to King Henry VIII of England. But do you notice anything else about them?''

I watched while the whole list moved rapidly past. ''Well, I can't really read them. They go by too quickly. But I can't say I notice anything in particular."

"That's probably because it's too obvious," said Nigel with a grin. I gave him a little smack. "Ouch! Okay, but you really did have the chance to see what I was getting at. You remember we talked earlier about an interpreter?"

"Oh! Oh, of course, how stupid of me. They're all in English!"

Nigel beamed. The slow pupil had finally gotten it. "Right. Now look at this." More clicking and typing. "You see, I've typed in exactly the same words I did at first. King Henry VIII. Now watch." He clicked the mouse button.

Instantly the screen changed. A list appeared in several columns of small print. I could read only a few of the words on the screen. The others were in languages, even alphabets, of which I knew nothing.

"Is that Japanese?" I pointed.

"No, that's Korean. That's the Japanese, there. But don't ask me what all the others are, because I haven't a clue to most of them. Choose one you're able to read."

"Goodness, I feel like an ignoramus. I don't know any of them! Except French. I used to be sort of good at that in college."

Nigel moved the arrow to the word *Français* and clicked. Again with no pause the screen filled with what I could, with difficulty, read as references to "le roi Henri VIII d'Angleterre."

"Now," said Nigel, who was clearly enjoying his demonstration immensely, "you do it." He relinquished his chair and sat me down in it. "Move the cursor—that's the arrow, you move it by moving the mouse—"

"I *had* figured out that much," I said rather acidly.

"Good for you." Nigel grinned. "Move it to that icon there."

"Icon?"

"The little pictures. They're symbols—"

I just looked at him.

"—as I'm sure you've realized," he went on in a hurry. "Go ahead, click the left button twice."

The little picture in question was a silhouette of two faces, nose to nose, like the old puzzle picture that could also look like a vase. I did as I was told.

The words on the screen shivered, became muddled, and then cleared.

They were all now in English.

"In other words," I said slowly, "I could look up anything in English and find all sorts of information in lots of other languages. And then have it translated back into English."

"And that's only part of it," said Nigel. "I could have entered the search in any language, not just English, and got the same results. Not only that, but even though I can't tell which is which, I know what a lot of the languages are." He took the mouse from me and made the computer return to the screen with all the listings. "That, I think, is Hindi. I'm pretty sure that's Sanskrit, and somebody told me that's Urdu—or maybe it's that one."

My mind had begun to work at last. "The languages of the developing countries. Nigel, now I understand what Bill Monahan was telling me. This could be a very important tool for people in these countries! Even if they don't read and write English well, they could get all kinds of information from English sources. And French, and Japanese, and—the mind boggles! This could open up the world for them!''

"And there's one last feature that really put this little gem over the top. Suppose you're in business in, let's say, Zaire. You intend to develop a source of—of something valuable, gold or uranium or zinc or diamonds or I don't know what. You need information about, perhaps, world legislation with regard to mineral rights. But for obvious reasons you don't want anyone to know what you're looking for. Almost any other information source can be traced. Phones can be tapped, library records can be searched, paper leaves a trail.''

"I thought the Internet was pretty easy to invade," I objected. "I may not know much about how it works, but I'm sure I've read about privacy concerns.''

"And you're quite right. Except, not when you're using the Multilinks search engine. It's encrypted, with an absolutely unbreakable code. I had to use a code to get into it just now, and nobody—repeat, nobody—except me can ever find out that today I looked up Henry VIII.''

"And nobody would ever know that the man in Zaire was checking on mineral rights. Or,'' I said, my voice shaking a little, "on how to stage a coup, or build nuclear weapons.''

"Yes. Now do you begin to see why Bill Monahan was on his way to being Mr. Megabucks? And why you may have got yourself straight into the middle of a hornet's nest?"

"Yes. Now do you begin to see why Bill Monahan was in the way, or not? Mr. Meyabecks? And why you may have got yourself caught into the middle of a hornets' nest?"

FIVE

HE SAT BACK, stunned. "There's something I haven't told you, Nigel," I said finally. The words came out as a shaky whisper. I cleared my throat. "Someone tried to break into my house last night."

"What!"

I nodded. "I thought—the police thought—it was just a burglar. He didn't get in. We have deadbolt locks. Well, that's what we call them in America, anyway—the kind that need a key from either side, so even when he broke the glass in the kitchen door—"

Nigel groaned, his head in his hands. "Why didn't you tell the police about your dead man?"

I noted that Nigel, too, was beginning to assume my ownership of a corpse. "I didn't know last night that there was anything peculiar about his death. I still don't *know* it, if you want to pick nits. He might have died a perfectly natural death. The only suspicious circumstance is that the doctor person, whoever he was, didn't report anything."

"He did more than not report the death," Nigel argued. "He must have spirited Monahan away somehow, or the body would have been found right away."

I was grimly amused. Nigel was now trying to convince me we were dealing with murder. "I wouldn't have thought disposing of a body was a one-man job," I said, playing devil's advocate.

"Oh, no, he had to have help. Two people could drag a dead man through the station and pretend the poor chap was royally pissed. It wouldn't be easy, but it could be done." Nigel sounded as though he had some experience, and I supposed he did. Not with the dead, presumably, but with the dead drunk.

"Well, but the real question is, why would someone want Bill Monahan dead? That's what we're going to have to find out."

And the argument began.

"Oh, no, you don't!" Nigel climbed onto his high horse. "You can't keep on getting yourself involved in murders. It's dangerous—haven't you learned that by now? Look here, did the man on the train, the bogus doctor, know your name?"

"Well, yes. I told him," I said in a small voice. "And where I lived. Looking back on it, I suppose it was a stupid thing to do, but I was trying to be helpful."

"Then it's obvious who your burglar was last night. They've warned you off. Face it, Mrs. Martin, they came to your house and tried to kill you!"

I took a deep breath. "I don't think so, Nigel. No, listen for a minute. I really don't see it. If these people wanted me dead, I think they're smart enough that I'd be dead. I think they wanted to scare me, and heaven only knows they succeeded."

"Right. If you say so. They wanted to scare you

off, stop you pursuing this thing any further, and if I were in your place, I should do exactly as they suggested!''

"Would you?"

Nigel's temper may be hasty and his tendency to make the most of his charm deplorable, but he has some sterling virtues. One of them is that, when push comes to shove, he's almost painfully honest. His eyes avoided mine.

"All right, then!" he shouted after a moment. "No, I shouldn't. I should chase them to the ends of the earth. But I'm not..."

He looked directly at me then, and trailed off.

"You're not an old woman. Is that it?"

"Look here, I—"

"It's all right, Nigel. I understand. You mean well. You're a kind child."

I saw him wince.

"You see? You don't like being condescended to, either. Now let's dispense with the protective nonsense. This is the way I see it. These people, whoever they are, are smart, but they've made one terrible mistake."

"It appears to me that they've covered their tracks admirably."

"So far they have, yes. You're absolutely right. The mistake I refer is their initial one. They killed someone."

Nigel glared. "That's a crime, a sin if you like, not a mistake."

"It's both. It's the one unforgivable crime. A murderer, even in today's corrupt society, has the whole force of law and order arrayed against him, for the rest of his life. It's a formidable force, Nigel—not just the police, but every single individual who respects the law, all lined up in opposition to our murderer.

"And he knows it. The very first reaction of a murderer to what he's done is fear and the desire to escape. That, Nigel, is the best weapon we hold, those of us on the other side. The murderer's fear works for us, because it leads him to do stupid things, unnecessary things, things that will, almost always, lead him into the snare that's set for him."

"'Almost' always," said Nigel, still angry and stubborn. "And what about the other people he kills along the way?"

"That, of course, can happen. It's one of the truly frightening aspects of murder, how often one leads to another. But that's just one more reason to act, and to act fast. Now look."

I changed my tack. "You're worried about me, Nigel, and that's sweet. I appreciate your concern, I really do. But I think you have the wrong idea about my intentions. I don't plan to go off in all directions and tilt at windmills. I'm going to be logical about it and use the resources at my command. And frankly, the most important of those resources just now is you."

I pointed to his computer. "You have there the most powerful information-gathering tool the world has ever known. I'd heard that said before this afternoon, but I didn't really understand. Now I'm a true believer. Why can't we—or actually, why can't *you*— use that tool to find out things they—the bad guys, whoever they are—don't want us to know?''

"For example?"

"For example, what's going on in Multilinks International that made someone kill their CEO?"

"And how am I meant to do that?" His anger had simmered down to sulkiness and sarcasm.

Good. That meant all I had to do was flatter him a little more, and he'd capitulate. "Heavens, I don't know! You're the one who knows how to make that box turn cartwheels. I hesitate to suggest it to some-one of your age and rebellious tendencies, but are you averse to doing something slightly illegal?"

That did it. He fought hard to hide the grin, but the dimples gave him away. "Meaning what?" His voice was meant to be gruff, his tone sober. He didn't quite manage it.

"I want you to break into the Multilinks computer. Hacking, I think it's called?"

"Holy—!" He omitted whatever word he'd in-tended, deferring at the last moment to my aged fe-male sensibilities. "It's called cracking, and it's rather more than slightly illegal, you know!"

"Oh, is it? I thought people like you, computer sharks, I mean, did it routinely."

"We-el…"

"Can you do it?"

He shrugged elaborately. "Depends. If their inter-nal security is as good as their Internet encryption, no. Nobody could, without a lot of very specialized and high-priced software, and maybe not even then. But it's rather surprising how often computer companies don't have good security. The cobbler's children, you know.''

"Will you try? Considering that we're strictly on the side of the angels?''

"And if I'm caught?''

"You'll have to make sure you aren't,'' I said flatly. "But I wouldn't think it was at all likely. They don't know you exist, for one thing, which should make it a lot safer. And it's not as if you were going to steal something. I only want you to nose around.''

"You know, Mrs. Martin, when I first met you, if anyone had told me you would one day ask me to commit a crime, I'd have wondered what they were smoking.''

"It just goes to show that first impressions can be deceiving, doesn't it? And if we're going to be partners in crime, I do think you'd better start calling me Dorothy.''

FEELING MUCH HAPPIER now that I'd enlisted Nigel's aid, I went home to plan the next stage of operations. I was really only one tiny step forward. I now knew who the dead man was.

At the thought, some of my mild euphoria evaporated. This was a really dangerous situation I'd gotten myself into. Why on earth couldn't the victim have been some simple tourist who wouldn't matter much?

"Dorothy Martin, you should be ashamed of yourself!'' I said aloud. Emmy, napping nearby, twitched a whisker but didn't wake. She was used to hearing her human talk to herself.

Any person's death was important. "Any man's death diminishes me...I am involved in mankind...send not to know for whom the bell tolls...." The venerable dean of Paul's had it right. I would, or I should, have been concerned, no matter who the victim was.

On a less philosophical note, if the man in the train hadn't been who he was, he almost certainly wouldn't have been murdered. Unless, of course, he was killed simply for his money and passport.

Oh, right, and then the casual killer is going to remove the body, at great inconvenience, and then try to break into your house. Very good, Dorothy.

I'm tired, I excused myself to my sarcastic alter ego. I hadn't had enough sleep, and my leg still hurt. I went out into the kitchen, made myself some coffee, and then curled up on the couch and turned back to my real problem.

Which, oddly enough, was an ethical one.

Was I going to get in touch with the police again and try to tell them my story, or not?

I shouldn't, really, even have asked myself the question. I was a conservative, middle-aged (at least) woman who had been brought up to think of the police as my friends. I was, for pity's sake, married to a policeman! My respect for the English police knew no bounds. I had information they needed. Of course I should tell them.

And yet...

I'd tried to tell them once and had met with nothing but obstruction. Of course, I hadn't known then who the victim was.

And you still don't know. You're guessing.

Deducing, I retorted, but that ruthlessly practical inner voice was right. I had no proof that any policeman would accept. Alan, who knew the way my mind worked, would have followed my reasoning and thought it worthy of at least some investigation, but Alan wasn't a working policeman anymore, and more to the point, Alan wasn't here.

It was reasonable to suppose that whoever killed Monahan was connected with his company. If I told the police I was sure he was dead, and they did take me seriously enough to look into the matter, they'd talk first to the London office of Multilinks International. Suppose by some chance they talked to the murderer. Of course he'd deny that Monahan was dead, or even that he was in England. I would be made to look like an idiot, the murderer would be warned, and I'd be in great danger.

The English police, by and large, are wonderful, but even they can't be everywhere at once. Could they protect me if the murderer found out I'd talked to them? Especially if they felt I was imagining things, and there was no threat against which I needed protection?

The police would tell me that they'd keep their source of information confidential, and most likely they would.

And yet...

Multilinks was evidently an outfit with money. Money buys many things. It has even, on occasion, been known to buy policemen. Not as often in England as in America, perhaps, but was I willing to take the chance?

I could report the matter to someone in Sherebury. That person would in turn report to someone at Scotland Yard, who would pass the information up to a superior, and so on.

Could I be sure that no one along that chain, no one answering a telephone, no one sitting close to someone else's desk, no one in command, was in the pocket of a rich American company?

I was being paranoid. All right, I'd continue to be paranoid. If I couldn't find out anything on my own, I'd talk to the police. But for now I was going to play a lone hand, and be damned to it! If that was a stupid decision, so be it. Having made it, I just had to make sure I went about the thing as intelligently as possible.

There was one other person who could help me, I decided after some intense thought. Just one who had the expertise I needed and whose discretion I could trust utterly. I picked up the phone and called London.

"Dorothy! How *wonderful!* I've been meaning to call you! It's been a *hundred* years since we've seen you and Alan."

Darling Lynn! She never changes, never loses that emphatic enthusiasm. It was nice to hear an American voice for a change.

"It has been a while, hasn't it? Listen, Lynn, I've been thinking about coming for a visit. Alan's away, and I'm bored and lonesome. Nothing like inviting myself, I know, but—''

"*Don't* be silly. You know we'd love to have you. What's Alan up to now?''

I told her, trying to keep my voice casual, but Lynn has known me for a long time.

"Poor you! You miss him a lot, don't you?''

"Oh, I'm all right. It's just that Zimbabwe is awfully far away, and it seems farther when I can't even visualize what it's like. Africa is so different from any place I've ever seen.''

"Parts of it, yes, but some of the cities are very modern, you know. Look, why don't you come tomorrow and stay as long as you want? Because Tom took *hundreds* of pictures the last time we went on safari. We'll show you Africa till you scream for mercy!''

An open-ended invitation. Perfect. I might be able to get all the information I wanted in a day, but it could take longer. I'd give myself some leeway. "You're an angel, Lynn. I can stay over the weekend, if you can stand me that long.''

We settled which train she would meet in the morning, and I hung up and began to think about packing. I'd have to take some of my nicest summer clothes. Lynn and Tom Anderson are delightful people, expatriate Americans like me, but they have a great deal more money than most people I know, and they live in a very fine house in Belgravia. When I visit them, I always feel I have to live up to my surroundings.

Then there were the cats to worry about. After supper I went across the backyard and knocked on Jane's door.

"Wondered when you'd turn up," Jane growled. "Losing my reputation. Burglary right next door, and I don't know all about it yet."

Beneath the growl there was a twinkle. Jane's reputation as Sherebury's one-woman news bureau was perfectly secure.

"You know as much as I do," I protested. I was getting a lot of practice in lying lately, and I'd get a lot more, I suspected, before this was all over. But what Jane didn't know couldn't hurt her—or me. "The police think it was an attempt at burglary, but he—well, or she—whoever it was—never got in, you know. Those new locks Alan had installed are really good."

"Mmm. Dodgy sort of burglar, to choose the oldest, smallest house on the street. A bit off, don't you think?"

"I did think so, and I said so to the police. But maybe it's because I'm at the end of the street, with only you on the one side and the cathedral on the other. My house is less likely to be observed," I improvised. "Or maybe they thought an old house might have simpler locks. Heavens, I don't know how a burglar's mind works! I'm just glad they didn't get in. It was bad enough that they broke the glass."

I was talking too much, explaining too carefully. Jane knows me nearly as well as Lynn does, but Jane is willing to bide her time. She gave me a sharp look, which I ignored, and offered me tea or sherry.

"Nothing, thanks. I can't stay. I have to pack before supper, and I plan to get to bed early, since I'll be up at the crack of dawn tomorrow. I'm going to London."

"Again? You went yesterday."

"I'm getting to be a gadabout in my old age. No, but yesterday was business. This is pleasure, or recreation anyway. I'm feeling a bit nervy, what with Alan gone and the burglar and all, and I decided I'd go see Tom and Lynn for a while. I wondered if you'd mind looking after the cats and keeping an eye on the house for me? I suppose I shouldn't leave you with that burden—I mean, with burglars around…"

I trailed off artistically, hoping to distract her from any further inquiry into the exact nature of the burglars. It worked, too.

"Hmmph! Suppose you think I can't deal with a burglar. Between me and the dogs, we'll cope."

I was profuse in my thanks, and Jane, who becomes deeply embarrassed by gratitude, shooed me out the door. "Enjoy yourself. By the way, did you ever find out who your dead man was?"

"Oh. No. There wasn't anything in the papers this morning, either. I do appreciate your doing this for me, Jane. I'll drop off the key in the morning before I go."

I got out of there as quickly as I could, aware with every step of Jane's gimlet eye boring into my back.

SIX

ALAN CALLED just as I was finishing my sketchy supper.

"Hullo, love. Thought I might hear from you last night. How did you fare with the doctor?"

"I meant to call, but it got late before I noticed. I'm free, Alan! No more cane, no more restrictions!"

"Splendid! No more pain?"

"We-ell. When it rains. Which it's been doing all day."

"I envy you. It's unbelievably hot and sunny here. Doesn't even cool down at night. One enjoys it for a little while, by way of contrast, but I've had enough."

"So when are you coming home?"

"Not for a bit, I'm afraid. The conference officially ends on Saturday, but the police wallahs here have asked me to stay on for a few days, to give them some advice on setting up a police college, and I've agreed. They've no sort of budget at all to hire consultants, you know."

What I knew was that Alan was a softie when it came to people needing his help. I admired him for that, but just now I could have done with a little more selfish attitude on his part. I wanted him home; I also needed his help. Of course, he had no way of knowing that, and I didn't want to explain my problem over the telephone, particularly not an international call. Satellite transmissions aren't exactly secure.

So all I said was, "I miss you. It seems like you've been gone for centuries."

"I know. For me, too." His voice softened. "If you'd rather I came straight home—"

"Of course I'd rather, but I don't intend to be one of those wives who order their husbands around. Not that I think I could get away with it, anyway."

He chuckled.

"So you go ahead and do what you need to do. Just be as quick as you can about it, will you, love?"

When he hung up, I felt lonelier than ever. A voice over a wire is a poor substitute for a real live huggable husband. And the satisfaction of having kept a stiff upper lip and been a brave little woman and lived up to all the other maddening clichés doesn't help much to keep one warm in bed.

The rain, which had moderated to a gentle but persistent drizzle, changed again during the night to a howling thunderstorm that woke me and the cats. I was very grateful for the new roof on my house; the old one had leaked. New windows also helped keep the weather on the outside where it belonged, but nothing could keep out the noise. After a while I went back to sleep, rather enjoying the storm. England's moderate climate doesn't often produce such humdingers. I was reminded of my Indiana home, where we used to get storms like this all summer long. The cats didn't share my enthusiasm. In their fright they snuggled up so close to me they nearly shoved me out of bed.

The rain kept on unabated into the morning. It obscured my vision as I drove to the station, and washed the train windows (which badly needed it) all the way into Victoria. I was able to avoid conversation with my fellow passengers, since the train was made up of antiquated rolling stock, the kind with separate compartments, and no one else was sitting in mine. I usually enjoy company as I travel, but given what had happened last time, I was grateful for solitude.

It was Tom who was waiting for me on the platform, not Lynn. "I'm taking a few days off in your honor, D.," he explained as he stashed my suitcase in his trunk. "Lynn seemed to think my sparkling company was required to keep you entertained."

"That's wonderful, Tom!" My enthusiasm was genuine, and not only for the sake of Tom's company. I was eager to talk to him privately and let him decide how much to tell Lynn, and the drive would give me the chance I needed. It was less than five minutes to the house, though, so I didn't beat around the bush.

"Listen, Tom," I began the moment we rolled away from the station, "I have an ulterior motive for this visit. I didn't tell Lynn, because there could be some danger involved. I don't have time to go into details before we get home, but to put it baldly, I think Bill Monahan's been murdered, and I need to know everything you know about Multilinks International. Look out!"

He swerved back into his lane, avoiding the big red double-decker bus by an inch or two.

"Remind me not to go driving with you again,

D.,'' he said mildly. ''Your conversation distracts a man's attention from the road. Why danger?''

''Because I've seen the murderer. I think. And he—or someone, anyway—tried to burgle my house Tuesday night. So they know who I am, and anyone I tell about it—well, you see?''

He was silent for a little while as he negotiated a couple of tricky corners, but as we pulled up in front of their house, he patted my knee. ''Tell Lynn and me the whole story. She'd never forgive me if I kept her out of it. And she knows how to keep her mouth shut.''

''It could be dangerous,'' I stressed again.

''The spice of life. What one of us faces, the other one does, too. That's the way it's been all our life.''

And there is a simple description of a successful marriage, I thought as I extricated myself from the car.

Lynn welcomed me with an enthusiastic hug, installed me in her luxurious spare bedroom, and then went downstairs to finish preparing an elegant lunch. I waited until we had given the meal the undivided attention it deserved before launching on my unpleasant agenda.

We had adjourned to the living room for coffee. Lynn was curled up on the couch, her legs tucked under her like a teenager's. Tom, in the rocking chair, was yawning. Putting down my coffee cup, I took a deep breath and began my story.

Tom and Lynn both listened with total concentration, saying not a word. When I had finished, Tom uttered a single low whistle, and Lynn let out a gusty sigh.

"What do you want us to do?" she said, clasping her arms around her knees. Her eyes were sparkling.

"You two are wonderful! No argument, no skeptical remarks, no overprotective concern, just an offer to help. I wish Nigel took this as matter-of-factly."

"He's too young," said Lynn. "Kids think adventure is their exclusive prerogative. It makes them feel insecure when we want a piece of it, too."

I considered that. "You know, I think it's more a kind of misguided knight-errantry. Although you may be right, too. Lord Peter Wimsey said once that the root of chivalry was a desire to have all the fun. Or something like that. Anyway, what I need now is mostly from Tom, I'm afraid, Lynn. I haven't thought of anything for you to do yet. But I'm in desperate need of information, and you, Tom, can get it for me."

"Sure. Like what?"

"To start with, I want to know what kind of trouble Multilinks is in. Are in? Whatever. See, Bill Monahan told me he was over here to look into a problem. The way I see it, it must be a doozy of a problem, or he wouldn't have come himself."

"I'd say you're right."

"Besides, he'd only been in the country two days. He said so. He'd never been here before. His murder has to be connected with Multilinks—he didn't *know* anybody else!"

"Dorothy, forgive me, but that *is* stretching a point," Lynn objected. "In the first place, you don't absolutely know he was murdered. He could have died of a heart attack or a stroke or something, and then had his body disposed of in a pretty unorthodox way.''

"Why would anybody go to all that trouble unless they'd killed him?''

She shrugged. "You're the detective. I'm simply saying your argument's not airtight, and it needs to be when you go to the police with it. Also, somebody outside Multilinks *might* have killed him, if he *was* killed. He could have friends over here, people he'd known in America who'd moved here, family—''

"Do friends kill friends?'' I demanded.

"Yes,'' said Tom and Lynn in unison.

I sighed. "Okay, okay, you're right. I'm theorizing ahead of my data. Sherlock Holmes warned against that. But I have to start somewhere, and Multilinks seems like the logical place. In fact, it seems like the only place, for a private individual like me. I can't go around taking fingerprints or interviewing witnesses. How many thousand people were in Victoria Station at about the right time, do you suppose? And how would I find them?''

"Okay, D., we take your point. I'll make a phone call or two and see what I can find out about Multilinks. Now, I don't know about you, but I'm ready for a nap after that lunch my lovely wife stuffed us with.''

Lynn threw a cushion at him and then yawned herself. "Power of suggestion,'' she said accusingly. "I'd planned a shopping expedition, Dorothy, but it's raining too hard. The perfect afternoon for a nap, in fact.''

We had our naps, and then we had a light supper, and then Tom and Lynn got out their pictures from Africa, and I was treated to a travelogue. The pictures were superb, taken by a man with a good eye and a wildly expensive camera. Lynn contributed a witty commentary, and I did laugh immoderately at the story of the night they were awakened in terror, in mid-safari, by unearthly yowls that turned out to be a couple of amorous tomcats. It was a long evening all the same. Tom had put in phone calls to some of his cronies and didn't expect any information until morning, but it was hard not to strain our ears, waiting for the phone to ring.

We finally gave up the pretense and went to bed. ''I'm not an early riser, Dorothy,'' said Lynn on the way up the stairs, ''but the coffeemaker's ready to go, and you know where the kettle is if you prefer tea. Just help yourself to anything you want to eat.''

''Oh, I don't expect I'll need anything, and anyway I expect to sleep forever. Thanks, you two. Good night.''

In fact, I slept badly. The nap had taken the edge off my need for sleep, and in the middle of the night the rain, that lovely soporific, stopped. In its wake came a heavy warmth that, again, reminded me of the summer humidity we sometimes had back home. The difference was that in Indiana there's always some air-conditioned place to provide refuge. Here it almost never gets anything like as hot, but to offset that, air-conditioning is very rare. I tossed amid my damp sheets. Finally, about five-thirty, I'd had enough. I crept down the heavily carpeted stairs to the kitchen and turned on the coffeemaker.

Tom walked in at six. "Wouldn't you know," he said grumpily. "Take the day off, could sleep in, can't sleep at all. We've got to air-condition this place."

"Have some coffee. I couldn't sleep either. It's cooling off, though. A breeze came up about a half hour ago."

The kitchen curtains were fluttering slightly, and the air was becoming fresher. I sat Tom down in front of the window and let the breeze and the caffeine improve his frame of mind. When he was on his second cup, I couldn't hold back any longer.

"Tom, what do *you* think is going on at Multilinks? Didn't anybody yesterday give you any idea?"

"Only rumors, D. An idea that there's something not quite kosher about the company, that maybe they're not doing quite as well as expected. I'll know more by noon, if there's anything to know."

We waited for breakfast until Lynn came down, and then sat around the house frankly staring at the phone. It rang, finally, three times in quick succession, and when Tom came back out of his study, Lynn and I pounced on him.

"Well, okay, I've got a little. Not a lot, but what there is, is somewhat surprising, I don't mind admitting. There's word on the street that Multilinks isn't doing very well on this side of the pond, and nobody quite understands why. They've got a hot product,

they've got good people, they've got the markets—
but they don't seem to be making much money.''

"Is somebody raking something off the top?"

"Not likely, according to my sources. That was my
first thought, of course. Seems like they're just not
getting the orders. If rumor is true, that is.''

"Do you think it is?"

"These guys have never led me astray before. Of
course, there's always a first time.''

"How about the company stock?" asked Lynn. "Is
it doing anything unexpected?"

"I don't know. My best stock-market tipster wasn't
available until this afternoon.''

"Then we might as well go shopping, Dorothy,''
Lynn insisted. "Sitting around here waiting will drive
us both crazy.''

She was right, of course, and it had been quite a
while since I'd had the pleasure of accompanying
Lynn on a shopping expedition. Her ideas on the subject are entirely different from mine. She loves an-
tiques and has the money to indulge her taste, so we
went to Christie's and Sotheby's and pored over cat-
alogues, stopped in a couple of charming little shops
in Jermyn Street, and ended up at Fortnum and Ma-
son's for tea.

"I do love Fortnum's," I commented as we walked
in the door. "It never changes. They can say what
they want about shopping from home over a computer, but just look—a computer could never replace
him!" I jerked my head toward a clerk in the tradi-
tional morning coat and striped trousers. Crystal chan-
deliers hung over the displays of foodstuffs, which

ranged from fresh fruit and vegetables so beautiful one might have thought they were made of wax, to mouthwatering smoked salmon and pâtés, to Campbell's soups in flavors like mulligatawny and vichyssoise. I sighed luxuriously. "My idea of the ultimate treat someday is to go somewhere wonderful and summery, like Glyndebourne, with some marvelous champagne and a hamper from Fortnum's. It sounds so thoroughly English and ever so slightly decadent."

"You're on!" said Lynn. "I've *always* wanted to do Glyndebourne myself, but Tom says picnicking on damp lawns in evening dress is not his idea of a good time, and he won't do it. We'll go, just the two of us, and have a lovely little party without the men. This *very* summer."

"It's a date." And we went upstairs to have a fabulous, and wildly expensive, tea, and to gloat over Lynn's purchase of a perfectly gorgeous old Wedgwood vase.

All the same, I was prickly with impatience to get back to the house and talk to Tom, and so was Lynn.

His news was interesting, but puzzling. He came straight to the point. "You asked about stock, Lynn, but it's no go. Multilinks hasn't gone public yet. They're expected to issue a stock offering soon, though, or they were. Now it seems the issue could be delayed, in view of their poor performance in the international market."

"Did any of your sources have any explanation for that poor performance?"

"Not a clue. The guys who know the most about it say a lot of potential customers came along and then just seemed to evaporate, lose interest, whatever.''

"These would be—who? What kind of customers? Individuals, or businesses, or—"

"Individuals wouldn't buy this software. It's way too expensive, up there in the thousands of bucks. Businesses, or government agencies. As you've realized, it's most useful to the developing countries, and they're the ones Multilinks came over here to woo. Apparently they're not impressed. At any rate, they're not buying.''

"Maybe they just can't afford it.''

"Maybe. The third world is poor; it's a truism.''

"But they would have known the price before they looked into it," said Lynn. "So why would they express interest and then go away?''

"Hmmm. Is it—the software, I mean—not as good as its reputation? Maybe these customers tried it and didn't like it.''

"No. I know myself that it's all it's cracked up to be. My company uses it; I've used it. It's saved us megabucks already, in time saved, mistakes averted, you name it.''

"Then why—?''

"You got me.''

We puzzled over it the whole evening, and for the rest of the weekend. I probably should have gone home, but I was genuinely weary and in need of a break, and I truly enjoy the company of the Andersons, who pamper me shamefully. By Sunday evening, nevertheless, I was counting the hours till I could get home and talk to Nigel.

SEVEN

"SO WHAT DID YOU find out?"

"Sod-all, I'm afraid. Oh, I got into their computer, it was dead easy. A six-year-old could have done it. But all I could find was boring official bumf. Sales records, expense accounts, personnel files, accounts payable."

It was late Monday afternoon, the first chance I'd had to sit down with Nigel at his computer. This time the Computer Centre was busy, but the students were working hard at various projects. Nigel's cubicle was somewhat set apart from the others. As long as we kept our voices low, we had reasonable privacy, though at this rate it looked as if we didn't need any.

I was crestfallen. It was at about this spot in the movie that someone who had been sitting for hours at the monitor should gasp and say, "Hey! Look at *this!*" And everyone would come running and watch, appalled, as the secret plans for the interstellar rocket appeared in detail on the screen. This was not working out according to script.

"Nothing? You're sure?"

"Nothing you want. I'm sure." Nigel took a swig from his bottle of designer water.

I sighed. "All right, then. Can you call up the sales records for me? I've been hearing rumors that sales aren't living up to expectations, especially sales in the countries that ought to be their best customers. Maybe if I looked at the records, I could figure out why.''

Nigel raised his eyebrows in one of those you-asked-for-it looks, shook his head sadly, and began punching keys. After a time a list appeared in front of me. It was perfectly clear, listing customer name, date of sale, item description, and cost. It told me absolutely nothing, except that Multilinks had in fact not been making a lot of sales. The total amount of money collected (or billed, I couldn't tell which) looked staggering to me, but I'm used to dealing with figures no higher than my modest checking account, so I'm no judge. Even I could see, however, that the dates of sales were widely spaced.

"Satisfied?"

"No. But I see what you mean.''

Nigel moved more or less at random through a few more Multilinks files. Accounts payable: suppliers, a cleaning service, a temporary help agency—nothing useful. The salary record was of interest only for the wide range represented.

"They'd have a fit if they knew we were looking at this,'' I commented idly.

"You've got that right. Everybody wants their salary kept confidential.'' He was about to move on, but suddenly I stayed his hand on the mouse.

"Wait, Nigel! Let me look at that again, from the beginning.''

He shrugged and moved the cursor to the top of the file.

"Do you have a pad and pencil?'' I asked, elevating my chin to peer at the screen through the bottom of my bifocals.

"What for?"

"I want to copy these names down. It isn't a very long list, just one, two…nine of them altogether, and I've just realized that with the salary figures, we've got a company hierarchy here. That guy must be the boss, see? Walter Spragge. He makes by far the most money. And this one must be his second in command, and so on. It might be useful to have these names— what's that?"

"The list," Nigel said patiently. "I printed it out while you were talking."

"Oh." One-upped by technology again. I do hate being made to remember how old and out of date I am. "Well, fine. Now, if I had some phone numbers to go with these names—"

"Personnel records. Coming up." He printed it without even asking. "Now, Mrs.—Dorothy, I'd like to get out of this, if you don't mind. The longer I'm in their files, the better their chance of catching me at it."

"Oh, heavens! Yes, get out right away!" Nigel's screen returned to its normal list of choices ("the main menu," he had explained), and then after a moment or two began to display a brilliant array of fish, swimming amid waving green fronds.

"Screensaver," he said in response to my querying look. "It isn't good for a screen to sit displaying the same image all the time—burns it in. So there are moving patterns available, like this one. I rather like it."

"Mmm." I pored over the lists in my hand. "Nigel, we need to find out something about these people. I'm sure Spragge must be the boss—the manager of the London office."

"Managing director, he'd probably be called," said Nigel, nodding. "And this Hugh Fortier, he'd be the assistant to the director. The others—oh, sales staff, probably, a couple of secretaries, an accountant. Not easy to tell which are which from the salary figures, except that this one must be the lowliest secretary." He pointed to the name Peter Grey, with a salary figure that would be adequate in my part of America, but in London, where living expenses are extremely high, would be meager in the extreme.

"He might be willing to talk," I mused. "He couldn't have much company loyalty, being paid a pittance like that."

"Unless of course he's a ghost employee, on the payroll but doing nothing at all. He'd not be likely to spoil a sweet arrangement like that."

I looked at Nigel in admiration. "You're getting good at this! I never would have thought of that."

"You have one great handicap as an investigator, Dorothy," he said with a disarming grin. "You assume people are honest."

"It is a limitation," I admitted cheerfully. "However, now that I think about it, the fact is that most people *are* basically honest. You get the twisters, of course, who automatically choose the dishonest way to do anything. And then there are the pathological liars. They don't always even know they're making it all up. But for the average person, going about life in straightforward fashion and following the rules is much easier than thinking of a good scam or a convincing lie.''

"If you say so.''

"I do say so. At any rate, the assumption works well enough as an operating procedure. You call it a handicap; I call it my biggest strength. I take people at face value, you see, which usually makes them like and trust me, so they talk to me. Which gets me back to the problem at hand. Nigel, I have to talk to these people.''

"Oh, no! No, tell me we're not back to that again! Look, Dorothy, show a bit of sense. You think one of these people is a murderer. Just what do you plan to do, ring them up and ask them if they did it?''

"Well, probably not. Though I might just surprise one of them into saying yes. Don't look like that; I was joking! No, but I want to—oh, I don't know, size them up, get a feel for what they're like. People reveal a lot when they talk. Seeing them in person would be better, but I know what you'd say to that!''

His blue eyes flashed dangerously. I pretended not to notice.

"So why don't we go to my house and make a few phone calls? We have their home telephone numbers, and they should be getting home soon. Who knows, I might get an inspiration, figure out some terribly intelligent question to ask them!''

"Why don't we do that?'' Nigel made it a question rather than a suggestion. He ran his hands through his thick dark hair, making it stand on end. "All right, I'll tell you why we won't do that. Number one, if you're right and the murderer is connected with the company, one of them might recognize your voice.''

"Oh. Yes. Well, then, you do the talking, and I'll listen.''

"Number two,'' he said, ignoring my suggestion, "what if they have caller display and they get suspicious? Then they have your telephone number. And number three—I don't need any more reasons, it's simply too dangerous!''

He sat back and crossed his arms, and I sighed, wishing Nigel would stop trying to protect me. Arguing wastes such a lot of time and is so exhausting.

"Nigel, I have the lists,'' I pointed out gently. "There is nothing you can do to stop me making some phone calls. If you're there with me, you may be able to make some suggestions or help in some way. I need allies, my dear, and I have only you and the Andersons! But if you'd rather not help, I'll do it by myself.''

I stood up. He swore under his breath and kicked at his book bag. "I can't leave until six,'' he muttered angrily. "And Inga's expecting me.''

"Don't worry, I'll call and tell her you're helping me. And I'll get the beer out of the fridge so it'll warm up nicely for you!''

When Nigel rang the bell about six-thirty, I was ready for him. After he had been placated with beer and a snack, I handed him a piece of paper.

"What's this?'' he asked suspiciously.

"Your script.'' I was rather proud of it.

He glanced at it, looked up at me, and read it aloud.

"'Good evening, John Smith here, financial reporter for the *International Herald Tribune.*' John Smith? *John Smith?*''

"Make up any name you like. I didn't take the time to work out a good one.''

"Impersonation is a crime.''

"Only if you're impersonating a police officer.'' I had certainly heard that somewhere. I hoped it was true. "Go on, read the rest of it.''

"'I wonder if you would care to comment on rumors that the stock issue Multilinks International had been planning has been delayed owing to internal problems.' That's it? That's all you want me to say?''

"At first. Then, if you can get them talking, I want you to ask about Monahan.''

"Are you totally bonkers? I can't do that!''

"All you have to say is that you'd heard Monahan was planning a visit to check on the situation himself. It should do the trick, don't you think? Get them talking? They'll deny it, of course. But the way they deny it will be interesting, and they may say something useful by mistake. You'll have to improvise, of course, make up replies to anything they may say. Have you ever done any acting?''

Nigel rolled his eyes. "In school plays I was always the spear carrier. Dorothy, I think this is a bad idea. I simply want to go on record as saying I think it's an extremely bad idea.''

"Duly recorded. Here's the telephone, and here's the list. I think you should start with somebody fairly unimportant to get warmed up.''

Muttering to himself, he picked up the list. "Very

well, then, I've said my prayers. Tell me who's the first victim.''

"This one. Evelyn Forbes. Fairly well paid, but not spectacularly. My guess is she's the boss's secretary. Have you decided who you're going to be?''

"Francis Evans. Frances was my mother's name. It'll do as well as anything.''

"What was her maiden name?''

"Robinson.''

"Use that, then. Just in case.''

"Very well. How are you going to listen in?''

"On the cordless phone. I have it right here.''

"No, don't use that. Cordless phones are essentially radios, no privacy at all. Isn't there an extension?''

"Only in the bedroom, and I want to be here.''

"Then you'll just have to share this phone. I hope it's loud enough. Are you ready?'' He picked up the phone and punched in a few numbers quickly.

"What are you doing? She's in outer London, oh-one-eight-one, not whatever you just entered.''

"Quiet.'' He was continuing to punch the buttons as he spoke. "That first sequence foils her caller display, if she has it. This number will be withheld. It's ringing.''

I leaned my ear close to the handset and listened while a woman answered with her phone number. Pleasant, brisk, efficient.

"This is Mrs. Evelyn Forbes?'' Nigel sounded efficient himself. The woman assented. "Good evening. My name is Francis Robinson, and I'm a reporter for the *Herald Tribune*. I apologize for ringing you at home, but I wonder if you could answer a few questions.''

"Questions? About what?" She sounded somewhat wary, but no more than I do when I suspect a telemarketer. "I don't wish to take in any more magazines—"

"No, no," said Nigel quickly. "I'm calling about Multilinks International. I understand you are executive secretary to Mr. Spragge?"

He had his fingers crossed, I saw. So did I.

"Yes, I work for Mr. Spragge," she replied after a pause. "What is this about, Mr. Robinson?" She'd gotten his name right, having heard it only once. I was extremely glad I hadn't let Nigel use his real name.

"There is a rumor circulating that the stock issue Multilinks had planned is now on hold, owing to internal problems. Would you care to comment on that?"

"Where did you hear that? And how did you learn my name?"

Sharp, defensive.

"We do not reveal our sources, Mrs. Forbes." He sounded so pompous that I had to stifle a giggle. "Is the rumor true?"

"I can't say anything about that. Excuse me, Mr. Robinson, but I have something in the oven—"

"May I ring up in the morning? At the office?"

"You may do anything you wish, but Mr. Spragge does not speak to reporters. Nor do I, sir." She hung up smartly.

"Whew." Nigel put down the phone and wiped his brow. "What a dragon! If they're all like that one—"

"You got by with it," I said. "She believed every word. You did very well, in fact, and we learned something."

"You may have learned something. I was too worried. I thought she was going to come right through the phone!"

"She was simply being the cool, efficient, protective secretary she is. Oh, I know a lot about her now. She's not young, she has an excellent memory, she's loyal to her boss and her company. Well done, Nigel! Now to the next one."

The next one was named Vicki Shore. She hung up as soon as Nigel launched into his spiel. Two of the men, Brian Upton and Peter Grey, reacted the same way, Upton with some juicy epithets before he slammed the phone down.

"Learning a lot, are we?" said Nigel.

"More than you might think. Learning a little about the people, anyway. Try this one again. He's the one whose phone was busy the first time."

This time Terry Hammond's phone rang, and he was much more forthcoming than the others. The trouble was that he said nothing to the point.

"Fine paper," he said with enthusiasm to Nigel's practiced opening. "How'd you get a job with sush a fine paper?"

"Well, actually, I—"

"Good job, is it?"

"Not bad. Now, about Multilinks—"

"I'm the bookkeeper. Keep the bloody accounts, don't I?"

"Then you must have some understanding of the financial position—"

"Financial pozh—pozhee—money. Not making any."

"Are you saying Multilinks isn't making money?"

"Hell with Multihowsyerfather. Me! I'm not making enough money to keep myself in drink." There was the sound of a hiccup. "'Scuse me."

Nigel rolled his eyes. "I've been told, sir, that Mr. Monahan may be planning a visit—"

"Who's he? Sounds Irish. The Irish know how to drink, I'll say that for them. Shay, would you care to come round? Make a party of it?"

"Thank you, no." Gently, Nigel replaced the receiver, rolled his eyes at me, and looked up the next number.

By eight o'clock we had only two names left on our list. Lloyd Pierce had been polite, but sounded distracted; a good deal of laughter in the background indicated some sort of party in progress. Chandra Dalal refused to talk once Nigel had said he was a reporter. That left the two highest-paid names on the list, the ones I assumed were the managing director and his assistant.

"Let's go to the top," I suggested. "Walter Spragge. What have we got to lose?"

Nigel tried the number. No answer.

"It's getting late, Dorothy. Inga…"

My heart smote me. I, too, was recently married, even if it was for the second time. And I could well remember my first marriage, and being young, and longing for Frank to come home from an evening class.

"There's only one more," I pleaded. "Then you can go home. The assistant manager, Mr. Hugh Fortier."

Glumly Nigel punched in the number. Without much hope I put my ear to my phone. It rang for a long time.

"He isn't home—"

"Fortier residence. Hello, is anyone there?"

Nigel, caught up short, stammered a reply. "Sorry—sorry. This is—is—" He looked at me, panic in his eyes.

"Francis Robinson!" I mouthed urgently.

"Sorry, swallowed the wrong way. Francis Robinson here, with the *Herald Tribune*. Mr. Fortier?"

"Yes." The monosyllable was not encouraging.

"I apologize for troubling you at home, sir, but I have been unable to obtain any useful information from anyone else, and I have a deadline to meet. I am attempting to confirm a rumor concerning the forthcoming Multilinks stock issue. I believe you are Mr. Spragge's assistant. Would you have any information about the offering?"

"I might have. What did you say your name was?"

"Francis Robinson. With the *Herald Tribune*."

"I see. You say you've called other people?"

"No one who could, or would, give me any answers. Mrs. Forbes refused to talk to me, and Miss Shore and some of the men hung up. Mr. Spragge was not at home." Diplomatically, he didn't mention Mr. Hammond.

"It's Mrs. Shore, not Miss," Fortier was saying. His voice had sharpened. "Just how much do you know about Multilinks?"

"Very little, sir; simply that a rumor is circulating that the stock will not be issued because of internal problems." I nudged him, and he went on, glaring at me as he spoke. "There is also some talk that Mr. Monahan has come to England to look into the matter personally."

Dead silence. Then Fortier spoke, in a voice that was little more than a whisper. "Just who the hell are you, and what do you want out of me?"

I jammed my thumb down on the disconnect button.

"Bingo! Nigel, we've done it! And am I ever glad they don't know who was calling!"

Nigel tried to glower, but a grin kept peeking through. "Got his knickers in a twist, didn't he?"

"So we were right! It *was* murder, and it is connected with Multilinks!"

"I wouldn't go so far as to say—"

"I would! That panic in his voice might not be evidence in court, but it's enough for me! Now all I have to do is prove it!"

"That's all, is it?"

"Nigel Evans, you should have been named Thomas! Doubt all you want to, but let me tell you something you don't know, my skeptical young friend. I think—I'm not quite sure, you understand—but I think Mr. Hugh Fortier is my doctor friend from the train!"

EIGHT

I SENT NIGEL HOME much later than I had intended. When this was all over, I would have to call Inga and apologize. But Nigel had been as eager as I to talk about the new development.

"How sure are you?" he asked for something like the fifth time.

"Nigel, I tell you I don't know! He had the same sort of accent, that's all I can tell you. The man on the train sounded vaguely Canadian, and so did Hugh Fortier. Fortier could be a Canadian name, of course, French Canadian. And he asked you something about 'calling' people, not phoning or ringing. That usage is more common on our side of the Atlantic. But it's none of it certain. Some of the others had accents, too—Mr. Hammond, for one."

"I've heard his sort of accent before," said Nigel with a snort of laughter.

"Besides drunk, I mean. But the ones who hung up—I really need to hear them talk some more."

"Oh, no, I'm not—"

"No, it doesn't have to be you the next time. I could call the Multilinks office and pretend to be from British Telecom, or the Inland Revenue, or something. Except I don't sound English, and I don't suppose Mrs. Forbes would let me through to anyone important. Or I could call some of them back at home, selling soap, or taking a survey. That's probably the best idea. I could phrase the questions so that the answers had words in them like 'out' and 'about.' You really can't mistake the way a Canadian pronounces those two.''

Nigel got a stubborn look in his eye, but I spoke before he could open his mouth.

"Nigel Evans, you are not to tell me I shouldn't get involved! I'm quite old enough to be your grandmother, and I won't have you telling me what to do and not do! Suppose you tell me where you'd be if I hadn't gotten involved with Canon Billings's murder?'' I didn't let him answer that one either. ''Oh, go along home with you! There's a beautiful girl waiting for you with dinner, and a few other things, I imagine. And don't look so shocked. I've heard of sex. Ask Alan.''

I was able to get him out the door on the strength of that astounding idea. I don't know why the young always think they invented it. Where do they think they came from?

I'd had my own supper hours before, so I was able to devote the rest of the evening to charting my new course. I knew perfectly well what I was going to do. The question was how to accomplish it. After considering and rejecting a number of ideas, I hit upon one that sounded feasible, and first thing in the morning I got out my address book, looked up the number, and called Tom Anderson at his office.

"Tom, I'm sorry to bother you at work, but I won't

be a moment. I find I must go to London this after-noon. I wonder, could I meet you somewhere for lunch to discuss the matter we talked about last week?''

"Of course. Let's see. Do you know the Sherlock Holmes pub in Northumberland Street?''

"Of course! What mystery lover doesn't?''

"That's not too far away from here, and you can get there easily by tube or taxi. One o'clock?''

"Wonderful.''

I do love a person who simply does what I ask without awkward questions.

The hours remaining before train time I spent pre-paring an approach and picking out one of my most becoming hats, a red one that most men love. Tom might have been cooperative on the phone, but I had the feeling I was going to have to do some fancy persuading, once he heard my idea.

He was waiting for me. He bought us each a lager and wouldn't let me say anything until I'd downed half of it in a few satisfying drafts. It was another hot day, and I was happy enough to drink my beer cold, for a change.

"Oh, but that's good. Tom, I'm sorry to drag you here in the middle of a day's work, but I couldn't very well impose on Lynn again.''

"Since when is a visit from you an imposition? Are you up to something sneaky you don't want her to know about, by any chance?''

"You know me too well. I don't think she's going to like what I propose to do, if you want the truth.''

Tom groaned. "That means I probably won't either. Well, let's have some lunch before you tell me. I have the feeling I'm going to need sustenance."

We ordered a ploughman's each; quick and good. I let Tom get some bread and cheese into him before I started in with a few feelers. "Tom, do you know what agency your company uses when you need temporary help?"

He blinked. "Are you looking for some help at home, D.? Because that'd be a different agency, you know."

"No, I know. But who do you use?"

He looked at me very suspiciously. I smiled and took another swig of beer.

"Oh, all right. We always go to Temp-Assist. We own them, in fact."

Eureka! That was the name I'd seen on the Multilinks accounts-payable list. Jubilation! I'd better try not to show it, though. I didn't want Tom to know Nigel and I had information we shouldn't have. If you're going to break the law, tell as few people about it as possible, is my motto. "I see. How convenient. It would be too much to hope, I suppose, that you know anybody there?"

He finished his beer in one long swallow and banged down the empty glass. "D. You said when you called that you wanted to talk about Multilinks. I am beginning to get a horrible suspicion, and I will not say one more word until you tell me what you have in mind."

"Oh, Tom, and I thought I was being so subtle! I

should have remembered that chess-playing mind of yours. All right, I suppose you've guessed that I want to get a temporary job with Multilinks. And I know I don't stand a chance without some help. And may I have another beer, please?''

The bar was very busy. I hoped by the time he came back with the beer, he'd have gotten used to the idea.

He had. He was also well prepared with ammunition against it. He set my beer down and became grimly businesslike.

''Now, first things first. Even if I liked the idea of your going in there headfirst—which I don't, not at all—it's impossible. You can't work in this country. Your volunteer job at the Cathedral Bookshop is one thing, but a paid position would be something else again. You need all sorts of permits and papers that you don't have. So it's impossible.''

He seemed very happy about it.

''Oh, but I thought of that. Of course I can't get paid. My idea is this.''

I hunkered over my beer in confidential fashion and lowered my voice. ''In America these days, more and more companies use temp agencies as employment agencies for the high-turnover jobs. Instead of going through all the hassle of conducting interviews and all that for their lowliest file clerks and so on, they just tell a temp agency what they need, and they know someone will show up every day, someone reasonably well trained and qualified. The company pays the agency; the agency takes a cut for its trouble and pays the employee. I assume it's much the same here?''

Tom nodded, frowning.

''Very well. Now, many of these jobs pay very badly and are very dull. I imagine that a young woman stuck in one of them wouldn't mind taking a week or two of paid vacation, would she?''

He was beginning to see what I was getting at, and though he still didn't like it, I could see admiration dawning grudgingly.

''You get the idea. You find out who the lowest of the low is at Multilinks and get her home phone number for me, through one of your contacts at Temp-Assist. I call her, tell her I want to take her place for a little while, for a bet. Almost anyone in England will do almost anything for a bet, I've noticed, and they'll believe the silliest things if they're told a wager is involved. We don't tell Temp-Assist a thing, the girl gets her money and her little holiday, and I get to do a little discreet spying. How does that sound?''

He buried his head in his hands. ''You have the most ingenious ways for getting yourself into trouble! I can think of a hundred objections!''

He couldn't, of course. In the end he could only come up with one, and that involved a minor detail, not a change in the basic plan.

''Temp-Assist will have to know. They check on the employees from time to time; it's part of their service. And if someone were to call Multilinks, and the girl wasn't there, she'd be in big trouble and you might be, too. If you're absolutely determined to do this—"

"And I am."

"—then you and the girl make up some story. She has a sick relative she has to go take care of, or whatever, and she wants you to take her place for a little while because she likes the job and doesn't want to lose it. You're probably her aunt."

"Great-aunt, I suspect. Clerk-typists come younger and younger these days."

"I leave you to work out the details. I'll still have to pull some strings, because they don't like to place anyone they haven't tested and trained, but I think it can be done. And it'll be safer that way, because Temp-Assist will know you're there and won't blow your cover."

"I can't use my real name, of course."

"No, that's right, somebody at Multilinks knows your name. But wait a minute, D.! They know your face, too, or one of them may. You can't possibly—"

"I thought of that, too. I'll wear a wig and leave my hats at home. There isn't a man in a thousand who can recognize a woman he's seen in a hat when she isn't wearing it, or vice versa."

I passed a satisfied hand over the current hat, and Tom smiled in spite of himself. It's really a very bright red, with a rakish little feather. Frank always loved it.

"All right, all right! I admit I almost didn't recognize you without a hat myself, the other day at our house when you'd just gotten up. I thought a strange woman was sitting across the breakfast table from me.''

"See? Anyway, big important executives don't notice a lowly temp.''

"Aha! And what makes you think your man is a big important executive?''

Oops! "Uh—he acted like one. On the train. When he was pretending to be a doctor.''

"You never were a good liar, D. What are you not telling me?''

"A few unimportant things, Tom Anderson, that I have no intention of telling you. You're better off not knowing. Now, I want to start work as soon as possible.''

He sighed heavily. "Yes, ma'am. I'll do what I can. By the way, do you by any chance actually possess any office skills?''

"Everyone in my generation learned typing in high school, and I've kept up with it a little. And anyone who's run a household for forty-odd years is an expert in organization. I'm polite and reasonably bright and can talk on the telephone. What more do I need?''

"Computer skills.''

"Oh. Oh, dear, I suppose you're right. Especially in a computer company. Well, I'll see what Nigel can teach me in a hurry. It can't be all that hard.''

It took another twenty minutes, and I had to switch to plain tonic or lose my reasoning edge, but Tom eventually came up with a plan. He had, as luck would have it, played golf with the CEO of Temp-Assist. He, Tom, would explain to his friend that his elderly aunt—I made him change that to middle-aged aunt—had made a bet she could make good in an office job, and he, Tom, needed some information and influence in order to help me out. When he got the information—the name of the employee and her phone number—he'd get in touch with me.

"How soon?" I said finally.

"*If* I can hook up with this guy, and *if* he can see me right away, and if we can get the information quickly—"

"A CEO can get anything done quickly."

"In theory."

"This is important, Tom. A matter, as they say, of life and death."

He sighed histrionically. "Yeah. Yours, maybe."

"How soon?"

"Couple of days, maybe."

"Tomorrow. And make sure it's a job that doesn't really need good computer skills, because I won't have the time to learn. File clerk or something like that."

"You know, the world lost a damn good executive when you took up schoolteaching! I'll do what I can."

"I'm sure you will, Tom. I don't know what I'd do without you." I smiled as winningly as I could, but Tom just laughed.

"Come off it, D. You've gotten your way. You don't have to turn on the megawatt charm. Will you beat me up if I tell you to be careful tomorrow, or whenever?"

"Why, suh, how you do go on! Fiddle-dee-dee!" I slid off the stool, batting my eyelashes for all I was worth as I headed for the door. When I looked back, Tom was shaking his head and looking imploringly heavenward.

Maybe southern belle wasn't my best role.

NINE

I SPENT WEDNESDAY buying a wig and a pair of glasses with gaudy rhinestone frames, and (sans disguise) talking Nigel into teaching me the rudiments of word processing.

"Why do you want to know?" he had demanded when I walked into the Computer Centre and made my request. "What are you going to do?"

"Ni-gel!" I split the word into two protracted syllables on a rising note loaded with vague but dire threat. Years of dealing with schoolchildren and cats had perfected the technique. I had actually intended to tell him what I was planning, but if he was going to launch into his protective mode, he could remain in ignorance. He started muttering to himself (it was becoming his standard response to my suggestions, I realized), but he sat me down at a desk and launched me into the secrets of typing at a television set.

At the end of three concentrated hours I knew how to create and save a document, how to find it again after I'd filed it, and how to edit it and print it out. And I'd fallen in love.

"But this is wonderful! So much easier than typing! Think of it, no more erasing or whiting over mistakes! I just overtype it, and it's corrected—amazing! And look at this—I can move a whole sentence around, or put in a word I forgot. It'll even show me my typos and look up synonyms for me! Why did no one ever tell me computers could do this sort of thing?''

''Wait till the hard drive crashes,'' said Nigel darkly. ''Or you forget to save a file and it's gone forever. Or the computer won't boot, or any of the thousand things that can go wrong.'' He was still annoyed with me.

''You can't fool me. You love these machines, or why would you be working with them?''

''I love them when they work properly. Half the time they don't.''

I gave him a very skeptical look.

''Okay. A quarter of the time. Some of the time. But what you must never forget is that a computer will not do what you want it to do. It will do only what you *tell* it to do. *Exactly* what you tell it to do, and only if it understands the command. *You* have to do the thinking. Never click a mouse button until you're quite sure you know what you're doing. Always—''

''Nigel.'' This time I was gentle, but firm. ''I think I've absorbed as much as my brain will stand for today. Thank you *very* much. One of these days I may actually consider buying one of these gadgets.''

I drove home absently, my mind full of strange new terms and my hands a little cramped from hours on a keyboard and mouse. Since Alan made me take driving lessons, I've been quite a bit more at ease on

English roads, but this afternoon I was so distracted I very nearly turned down the wrong side of my street.

There were two messages on my answering machine. The blinking light drove every other thought out of my head.

"You are to report to Temp-Assist at nine tomorrow morning." Tom gave the address in an extremely dry voice. "I had my secretary set the thing up with Alice Scott, whom you'll be replacing. I didn't trust you not to get carried away with the details. She was delighted, incidentally, Alice, I mean. At Temp-Assist they'll give you some instructions and send you on to Multilinks. Everybody and his Aunt Sally has protested about this, D. You're supposed to go through all kinds of testing and training and God knows what. The big boss had to talk, in person, to a lot of flunkies to get you out of all that, and he's taking a big chunk out of my hide for it. You'd better be good at your job, or I'll never hear the end of it. And D.—be careful."

My heart thumped uncomfortably in my chest. This was what I'd thought I wanted, but now I had it, that old adage about being careful what you pray for hit home with force. It had been many, many years since I'd had a new job. I had completely forgotten what it felt like. Anticipation vied with stage fright, anxiety and fear with hope, all doing a jig somewhere in the region of my stomach.

I wasn't young anymore. There was no denying it. I was about to go into a strange office in a country that, no matter how much I loved it, was not my own.

And to make matters much worse, I was going in there under completely false pretenses. I'd never worked in an office in my life; my career had been in the classroom. I'd have to pretend to know routine I'd seen only on TV shows and in the movies. I'd have to be professional and competent—not only, I reminded myself, to preserve Tom's reputation, but to save my own skin. There was a murderer in that office. I swallowed hard.

A cup of tea and several cookies later, I remembered to listen to the second message. It was Tom again.

"Almost forgot. Your name is Louise Wren. And you had your purse stolen two days ago and don't have new identification yet, just in case anyone asks you for some. They probably won't, but it's best to be on the safe side. Don't forget your name, and you'd better take a new purse to preserve the fiction."

Heavens, I'd never thought about anyone checking my identification! I broke into a light sweat as I thought of the terrible mistakes I could have made. What a good thing Tom was thorough.

I had two phone calls after dinner. I was in my bedroom, dithering about what to wear for my first day on the job and wondering just how early a train I'd have to catch, when the first call came in.

"Dorothy, it's Lynn. Now, *listen*. Tom's told me what you're doing. He didn't want to tell, but I made him. He may be able to keep secrets from *other* people, but they haven't been married to him for twenty-seven years."

"Oh, dear." I sat down on the bed. "I suppose you don't approve."

"I think it's *thrilling!* I'd have done it myself if I'd thought of it. Tom had a *fit* when I told him *that.* But he said you were going to be taking the train in to London every morning, and that makes no sense at all. Come and stay with us for as long as you need to. I *won't* take no for an answer."

"Oh, Lynn, I'd love to, and it's very kind of you to offer. But there's the house, and the cats—"

"You know *quite* well Jane will look after the house and the cats."

"Yes, but I don't want to explain myself to her. I do feel very strongly that the fewer people know about this, the safer we all are."

"Yes, I know. Make up something for Jane."

"I don't lie very well. It's an art I should cultivate, I know."

"I'll teach you. I lie *beautifully* in a good cause. Let's see. A friend from America has just arrived in London and wants you to show her around. Or your godchild is getting married a week from Saturday at St. George's Hanover Square. Her mother is *beside* herself and asking for you. Or your friends Tom and Lynn Anderson are going away and need a house-sitter. Or the Queen has invited you to a garden party, and you have to do some serious clothes shopping. Or you've decided to take up Zen, and someone has told you about a *marvelous* guru near Hampstead Heath. Need any more? I'm just getting started." She paused for breath.

I was laughing by that time. "No, I expect one of those will do. Lynn, you're wonderful. I'll see you tomorrow sometime, probably not until I get off work."

I settled for the godchild story as the likeliest and presented it, with some embroidery, to Jane. She accepted it with calm acquiescence, though she did not, I was sure, believe a word. Biding her time, that was Jane. Well, I'd tell her the whole story. Someday.

Alan, calling later, was harder to deal with.

"Alan! I'm so glad you called. I'm sorry I've been out of touch. I was going to call you, but I was afraid it was too late."

"Close on midnight, but we keep late hours here. It's too hot at midday to do anything productive, so we carry on the siesta tradition. Life takes up again somewhere about four, and goes on quite late. They view midnight as the shank of the evening."

"I thought mad dogs and Englishmen went out in the midday sun."

"Not this Englishman, not here. You're sounding a good deal more like yourself, I must say. I thought you were a bit under the weather last time."

"I'm feeling better; it finally stopped raining." We discussed that useful subject for an expensive minute or two. I've never gotten the hang of talking long-distance to someone I love. There's too much to say, so I end up saying nothing in particular.

"What have you been doing to keep yourself so busy you couldn't phone your neglected husband?"

Conversation is especially difficult, of course, when

you have something to hide. I'd been making little notes while we talked—things I could safely say. "Oh, this and that. I went to see Tom and Lynn last weekend. Lynn and I have decided to go to Glyndebourne this year. And oh, Alan, I've been having Nigel teach me to use a computer. It's fascinating!"

"A computer? Whatever for?"

"Because I was feeling old and didn't want to turn into a stick-in-the-mud, mostly. But now I'm beginning to think I might want one. I've learned a little about the Internet, too, and I'm hooked. Are they terribly expensive?"

That lasted us a while, too. Alan was beginning to sound sleepy, so I took a deep breath and dived in.

"Oh, I nearly forgot. I'll be in London for about a week, or maybe longer, starting tomorrow. Have I ever mentioned my godchild Crystal?"

Where that name came from, I'll never know. It was the first one that came into my head.

"I don't believe so."

"Well, I've been out of touch with her for quite a while. Crystal Redgrave. No, no relation, unfortunately—I'd love to meet *that* family! Her mother was one of Frank's students, and when she married and had a baby girl, we were the godparents. Then they all moved to England...." I went on for some time providing details of a fictional family who were beginning to seem quite real to me. "So, anyway, Crystal is getting married in a few days, and she and her mother want me there to help. They're sort of frantic, I guess, with a house full of guests. I'll be staying with Tom and Lynn again if you need me. Do you have their number?''

''Yes.''

Silence.

''Alan? Are you still there?''

''Yes.'' Pause. ''Dorothy, are you?—is there something?—I have the oddest feeling you're not telling me everything. You sound—different.''

Alan's naturally keen perceptions have been honed by long years as a policeman. His sensitivity is one of the reasons I love him so much.

Usually.

''I'm a bit distracted, that's all, love. This came up rather suddenly, and I've been running around trying to decide what to take and getting Jane to look after the cats and all. Really.''

''Dorothy, I wish—I'm sorry I can't be at home just now.''

''Me, too!'' And if that came out a little more like a wail than I'd intended, at least it had a positive effect. Alan dropped that speculative tone and became soothing, and I relaxed. He hung up after I promised to call him in a day or two.

I'd have to keep that promise, too, or he'd get really concerned. I hated lying to him, but I simply couldn't explain over the telephone. Besides, he'd worry, and he needed to keep his mind on his job. I wished he were here to help, but he wasn't, and that was that. I'd just have to do my best on my own.

I WAS UP at dawn on Thursday, having slept, between the rigors of packing and the prickles of worry, only a few hours. I called a minicab, having no wish to struggle with two large suitcases by myself or leave my car parked at the station for who knew how long. The cats were indignant. They don't care for disruptions in their routine, and they hate suitcases, whose implications they understand full well. The cabdriver was greeted by anguished Siamese howls and thought, I'm sure, that someone was being murdered. I donned my wig and new glasses in the cab, not wanting Jane to see them, and when an apparently strange woman climbed out of the cab, the cabbie's demoralization was complete. He deposited my bags and got away as quickly as he could.

The packed train got to London on time, by some miracle. But miracles don't often come in bunches, and they ceased when I got to Victoria Station. I had never before witnessed the daily commuter crush, much less tried to negotiate it. It was no place for a lady of mature years and a slightly gimpy leg. I stood helpless as the tide of humanity surged past and around me, running for the station exits, the escalators to the Underground, the taxi stands. I had planned to leave my luggage in the checkroom and take the tube to the Temp-Assist office. I altered my decision in thirty seconds flat. Forget the Underground. Across the station, down two escalators, through several short tunnels, into a sardine-can train, up more escalators, another walk—no, thank you. I would be doing very well to make it to the taxi stand in one piece.

I hurried through the station, got a cab without too

much delay, and took it as far as a traffic jam just around the corner from the Temp-Assist office. It would look more realistic, I felt, to arrive on foot. Louise Wren was not terribly well-to-do. I hoped I was coming from the right direction, as if I'd come from the Underground, but when I got to my destination, I realized that was the least of my worries.

The office was packed with young women, all dressed in the same uniform of short dark skirt, white blouse, and black high heels. Oh, the pattern of the skirts and blouses varied, as did the height of the heels, from moderate and almost comfortable to Grand Inquisitor. But there wasn't another soul in the place in a dress. And there wasn't one over thirty. Three of them were sitting together in a little knot near the door. They stopped talking when I walked in, looked up with mouth agape, and then went back to their conversation.

I was very sure I heard a stifled giggle.

TEN

I survived the condescension of the young job applicants in the Temp-Assist office and their ill-disguised astonishment when I was the first to be called to the desk of the woman in charge. I survived her scornful disdain. She plainly had no use for anyone who got a job by pulling strings. She was careful to make sure that, no matter who my friends might be, I knew who was in control of this situation.

"It is most irregular for us to allow anyone to work under our auspices, even briefly, without the necessary credentials. You have no identification papers, nor have you been tested. I can only hope that you will be able to carry out your duties properly. Our reputation is of the highest; bear that in mind. And you do quite realize that you will receive no compensation of any kind? So far as we are concerned, officially, Miss Scott is still the receptionist at Multilinks. Is that clearly understood?"

I humbly said that it was, and murmured something about emergencies that could happen to anyone. I was ignored.

"Very well. This is the address of the Multilinks office. The tube stop is Russell Square. Left out of the station, cross Woburn Place, second right is Northampton Way. They expect you at ten sharp."

She handed me a form, turned away from me, and, picking up another form, addressed the room at large. "Miss Hamilton, please." If she had literally washed her hands, she couldn't have made her meaning clearer.

I also survived the glares of the young things. "Well!" said one of them to her companion, in a voice meant to be overheard. "Seventy if she's a day—that wig doesn't fool me! *And* with an American accent! And will you look at those shoes! This agency isn't what it used to be!"

I survived all of these indignities, but I didn't enjoy them. My morale dipped lower and lower on the way to Multilinks. Once more I had hailed a cab as soon as I got out of sight. I didn't intend to start my new job by being late, or by looking decrepit, an effect that a run to and from stations would certainly create. Seventy, indeed! I pulled my shoulders back. It must be the wig. It looked, I was sure, very odd. And I felt naked without a hat, though the light brown wig was certainly hot enough to count as one.

At least I was going to a familiar part of London. Northampton Way was only a block or two away from Russell Square, the heart of Bloomsbury. Frank and I had stayed once at the venerable, old-maidish Russell Hotel there, in the old days when he exchange-taught at the University of London and we used to haunt the British Museum. I loved Bloomsbury, with its neat white houses and shiny black railings, its unexpected little squares and gardens. On impulse I sat up and tapped on the driver's window as we were rounding Russell Square.

"Set me down at the corner, would you? I'll walk from there."

"Right you are, madam. Lovely day for a bit of a walk." His good cheer was probably enhanced by the fact that the corner in question was right in front of the big hotel, where he was guaranteed a quick fare.

I had fifteen minutes to spare. I spent five of them watching the activity in the square and regaining my composure. It didn't matter what those rude young women thought. I might be an American, but I had known London since long before they were born. I remembered things they had never seen—shillings and half crowns and great copper pennies, tea at Lyons Corner House, fish and chips wrapped in newspaper. I remembered sitting with Frank on a bench in the chill winter sunshine, on that very bench there, or its predecessor, on our very first day in London, all those years ago. We'd held hands in silence, drinking in the great city around us, too full of sheer happiness even to speak. We'd opened a small account at Barclay's Bank, that very branch I was looking at now, and had thought ourselves too cosmopolitan for words.

My memories made this place mine. London belonged to me as much as to the giggling girls in the office, as much as to the Arab and Indian and Chinese and Egyptian and Nigerian students who hurried past me, intent on reaching their lectures on time.

On time. Yes. Was I dillydallying because I had a little extra time, or because I was nervous?

Scared stiff would be more like it. I abandoned nostalgia with a sigh and got myself moving.

It was a clear, still day. Over the babble of street noise I heard Big Ben, only a couple of miles away, strike the four quarters as I turned into Northampton Way. By the first stroke of ten I reached the door marked Multilinks International and, obeying the instructions on the sign, walked in.

The front desk, located in a spacious black-and-white-tiled foyer just beyond the entrance hall, was unoccupied. That was no surprise, since I was destined to be its next occupant. I had been told to ask for Mrs. Forbes, who was, as Nigel and I had guessed, the boss's secretary. I was wondering whether to knock on the door out of the foyer, when it opened and Mrs. Forbes came out.

I knew it was she before she spoke. She matched her telephone voice perfectly. Well dressed, well groomed, poised, and—bless her—in her late fifties, at a guess.

"Good morning," she said pleasantly. "You must be Miss Wren. Or is it Mrs. Wren?"

After a very trying day so far, the gods were beginning to smile once more. I had been ready to introduce myself as Dorothy Martin!

"Mrs. Wren. I'm a widow."

"American?" she said with a little frown.

"American-born, but I've lived in England for quite some time. I can't seem to lose the accent."

"I see. Well, you'll not feel alone; there are a good many accents here. We've a South African, an Indian, and three Canadians, as well as the English, of course. We also have clients from many countries phoning in. Can you sort them out, do you think?"

"That shouldn't be a problem. I admit to having a little difficulty with Scottish accents sometimes, especially people from Glasgow."

"Oh, well, no one can understand *them*, can they?"

We both laughed; I relaxed a notch.

"I must say it will be awkward doing without Miss Scott. She has been here for some months and is very efficient. However, family crises can't be helped, and I'm sure you'll soon learn our way of doing things. Your duties are quite simple, really. There's very little word processing; Mr. Grey and I handle that, except for the odd memo now and again. You will answer the telephone and route the calls. I've made you a list of the people here and what they do, so you'll know who can deal with a caller who doesn't specify a certain person." She handed it to me. "We're quite a small office, you see. The three sales staff are rarely here, though they receive a great many calls. You will have to be very careful about their messages."

"Of course. Lost messages lose sales."

"Quite right. Then the assistant director, Mr. Fortier, is also out a good deal."

"Fortier?" I said quickly. My voice came out as a near-squeak; I lowered it a trifle. "That's an unusual name. My late husband and I used to know some

Fortiers. That was back in America, but they were Canadian.''

''Mr. Fortier is Canadian, but I doubt there's a connection. Mr. Fortier is a quite a lot younger—oh, I didn't mean—''

''It's all right. I'm not as old as I look—it's this new wig, it wasn't a good idea—but I don't mind admitting to my age. I'm fifty-nine, but I know I look older. I've had a bout with cancer, and the chemotherapy hasn't been over for very long. The doctors say I'm doing very well, but it took a lot out of me, and my hair still hasn't grown back properly.''

All that on the spur of the moment! Apparently it was only with people close to me that I couldn't lie convincingly.

It went down beautifully. Mrs. Forbes didn't seem to boggle at my creative version of my age, but simply smiled with great sympathy. ''I hope you're doing well.''

''Feeling fine, thank you, but that's why I've had to take temporary work. My résumé isn't up to date, and of course at my age it isn't easy—''

''I know exactly what you mean! I feel very fortunate to have found such a good post here. I believe that in America there are laws about age discrimination?''

''There are. They're not very effective.''

''Here we haven't even the laws. But Mr. Spragge is marvelous to work for, and adamant that he prefers an older secretary, though we must take what we can get in the way of a receptionist.'' She turned slightly pink. "Oh, dear, I don't mean you, Mrs. Wren. It's these young girls..." She shook her head and clicked her tongue. "But for the money we can offer, of course the older, more highly qualified staff prefer to go elsewhere. And the turnover—but I expect you're not interested in our staffing problems. I personally think we're lucky to have you, and I hope you'll be happy here."

The telephone rang. "Oh, dear, here we've been chatting, and I ought to have been instructing you about the telephone. I'll just answer this, and then we can sit down and get to it, and I'll run over the computer and our filing system with you as well."

The conversation had drifted away from Mr. Fortier, and I saw no way to tug it back. Well, doubtless there would be other opportunities.

By lunchtime I had answered twenty-seven phone calls (I had to log them), taken fifteen messages, escorted three customers in to the sales secretary, Peter Grey, and filed half an in tray. I had also played around with the computer—which operated very much like Nigel's, to my relief—and had accomplished exactly nothing related to my real purposes. I was exhausted.

"Lunchtime, Mrs. Wren!" Mrs. Forbes came out of her office. "Mr. Grey very kindly takes his lunch late so that the receptionist and I can go out at one. Do you know the area, or would you like me to show you a café or two?"

"My husband and I used to know it at one time,

but I've lost touch. I'd be very grateful if you'd show me."

I couldn't, as her subordinate, suggest that we eat together, but I was delighted when she made the suggestion. "I'm a widow, too, and I know one gets lonely." Over salad and tea at a self-service café, I had the chance to ask her a few of the things I was longing to know.

"Could you tell me about the rest of the staff, Mrs. Forbes? I've met only Mr. Grey, and I didn't really get a very distinct impression of him."

She laughed a little. "Grey by name and gray by nature, I'm afraid. He's one of our Canadians. That is, he was born and raised there, so he has a bit of the accent. I imagine you caught that."

"I wasn't sure; it isn't very strong."

"No, he's lived here for a few years. His parents were English, I understand. I think he said he moved over here when they died. I don't quite remember; one often doesn't remember what Peter Grey says, I'm afraid. He's that sort of person. Fades into the wallpaper. Extremely efficient secretary, though."

"When you say he lives here, you mean here in London?"

"No—Surrey, I think. Perhaps even Kent. Again, I simply can't remember. I know he is sometimes late getting in to the office when the trains are delayed."

"As they so often are. Does that upset his boss, Mr.—oh, dear—"

"Don't worry, you'll have all the names soon. Mr. Upton, Brian Upton, the director of marketing. You

must meet him this afternoon. He's half Irish, you
know, and has a bit of a temper. He—well, you must
make up your own mind. I don't want to prejudice
you. But if I were you, I'd be careful to keep the right
side of him. He does get very angry with Mr. Grey
at times; he ruined his computer once—threw a pa-
perweight, and it hit the monitor. And it's so unfair.
Poor Peter doesn't drive the trains!''

Peter Grey, nonentity, Canadian; Brian Upton, capacity for violence. Nothing unexpected there, given
the brief phone contacts I'd already had, but I duly
filed them away. ''All right, let me see. Then there's
Mr. Spragge, of course.''

''Yes, I'll introduce you to him when he isn't busy.
He is a truly dedicated man, and the most brilliant
person I've ever met.''

There was a distinct note of awe in her voice. ''Is
he married?'' I asked, and could have bitten my
tongue. ''I'm sorry, I didn't mean—that is—''

She laughed. ''I have no designs on him, if that's
what you mean. No, I admire him intensely, but not
in that way. He's far younger than I, for one thing,
forty at a guess. And yes, he is married, with two
lovely children, teenagers, a boy and a girl. And quite
devoted to his wife, poor dear.''

''Poor dear? Mr. Spragge?''

''Sorry, I meant Mrs. Spragge. She's a virtual invalid. There was an accident, years ago, and her back
hasn't been right since. She is confined to a wheel-
chair nearly all the time.''

''Oh, dear! What a pity for such a young woman!''

"They manage. Mr. Spragge would do anything for her. He is a man of great compassion and integrity."

"I look forward to meeting him. Now, there are the three salesmen—"

"You won't see much of them, actually. And of course one of them is a woman." She snapped her mouth shut on further comment. I wondered what she wasn't saying, but for now I thought it was better to let her tell me just what she wanted to. Time enough to probe when I knew everyone better.

"Mr. Pierce is another Canadian. We've rather a lot of them; Multilinks is quite important in Canada. He's Welsh by descent, though, and looks it. One of those dark, brooding types. He's been in England for a year; I don't think he cares for it much."

"Does he live in the country, too?"

"Oh, no, London and the fast track for him!"

"Not married, then, I take it."

"He has a wife."

What an interesting way to put it. "Who else?"

"Mr. Dalal and Mrs. Shore."

"Mr. Dalal is Indian, I take it."

"English born, but of Indian parents. First-class degree in maths from Cambridge, but he preferred a sales post to teaching. He doesn't seem to get on well with the others—rather a pedantic little man. And Mrs. Shore—she prefers Ms., by the way, and one can see why. She is—very attractive. Red hair, that creamy sort of skin."

Again Mrs. Forbes closed her mouth firmly, and again I wondered.

"Is that all of them?"

"Not quite. The bookkeeper is Mr. Hammond."

Ah, yes, the bibulous Mr. Hammond.

"He works just round the corner from my desk, in that sort of cubbyhole off the main office. You'll see quite a lot of him, of course. He's South African."

"Black?"

"White. He disapproved of apartheid, back when it was still in effect, so he left and came to England. He makes us all laugh."

"A *bookkeeper?*"

"I know, odd, isn't it? So often they're such drab people, but Terry is funny. A bit too brash sometimes. Mr. Spragge gets irritated, but I think it's just high spirits."

Well, she probably had the spirits part right.

"That's the lot, except for Mr. Fortier, of course. But as I said, he's almost never in the office, so you'll see very little of him."

Well, that was both a blessing and a disappointment. If I never saw the man, how could I tell whether he was my murderer? Though if he was, it would be much better if he never saw me. I probed a little.

"He must be a very able man, to be second in command to Mr. Spragge."

"Oh, he is. Young, of course, but very eager to make good, and sensible enough to take Mr. Spragge's advice, which is more than I can say for some."

Ambitious and a yes-man. I put the information in

my mental file drawer and speared the last sprig of watercress.

Mrs. Forbes finished her tea and sighed. "I must go, but you needn't. Stay and have a sweet if you like. You're not due back until two."

I looked at my watch. It was only one-thirty. "Some shopping to do?"

"No, work at the office. Things have been—rather difficult of late, and I've got behindhand." She sighed again. "It used to be such a pleasant place to work, but lately everyone seems to be in a temper."

That was interesting, if not specific enough to be useful. "I might as well go with you. I certainly don't need any dessert."

We stood, and Mrs. Forbes dropped her handbag, a big carryall. A book fell out. I picked it up for her.

"Oh, John Buchan! I love him, especially *The Thirty-Nine Steps*. I haven't read this one, is it good?"

"Oh, yes! I do believe *Greenmantle* is my favorite, though I enjoy them all. I read a lot of thrillers from that period—Edgar Wallace, you know, and Oppenheim, though I think I like Buchan the best. I really prefer them to most modern writers."

"They're very exciting, aren't they? I've never read Wallace, but I'm just beginning to get acquainted with Oppenheim. Do you like mysteries—I think you call them detective fiction—or just the thrillers?"

"Oh, no, I love the Golden Age writers, Agatha Christie and Dorothy Sayers and that sort!"

"But that's how I first learned to love England, by

reading Agatha Christie! What's your favorite of her books?''

We talked popular literature all the way back to the office, and by the time we got there, friendly relations were firmly established.

Good. I was going to need a friend in this nest of possible murderers.

ELEVEN

THAT AFTERNOON I met Terry Hammond, the bookkeeper, a freckled, pleasant-looking man of about
thirty with lot of very red hair, worn rather long, and
a friendly, open face. I could see why Mrs. Forbes
liked him. He didn't, at a quick glance, remind me at
all of the man in the train. Surely I would have noticed the red hair, and even if I hadn't, under the hat,
I couldn't have missed the marked tremor of his
hands. He bore none of the other stigmata of the
heavy drinker, but a man with a problem is a man to
watch.

Nor did Brian Upton look like my train man,
though he did not impress me at all favorably. When
Mrs. Forbes introduced us, I got a nod and a growl
in response to my smile, after which he shouted for
Peter Grey and ignored me completely. I did get a
good view of his profile. He looked like a ferret. Had
the man in the train been at all like that? I simply
couldn't remember; all I could recall was a black suit
and a black hat and a stuffy sort of manner. Upton
did have the right sort of build, but not the right sort
of accent, so far as I could judge on the basis of a
snarled word or two.

The only other person working in the office that
day was Mr. Spragge. I'm not sure quite what I ex-

pected from Mrs. Forbes's gushing recommendation, but I know I was skeptical and certainly not prepared to be charmed. Perhaps it is a universal human reaction to bristle a trifle when one is told, "Oh, you'll love him!" At any rate, it is often my reaction.

I didn't meet him until it was nearly quitting time. I was ready to drop, to tell the truth, and I was discouraged. No matter how young I felt inside, my body was forcing me to admit that a full day's work, after several years of retirement, was a bit much. Not only that, I felt I had knocked myself out for nothing. No progress, not a single piece of useful information. So it was in no sweet mood that I accepted Mrs. Forbes's summons to "come in and meet our Director." I could hear the capital letter in her voice.

But charmed I was, almost in spite of myself. My new boss turned out to be an utterly delightful man, in appearance as well as manner. He looked a lot like an actor, whose name I couldn't remember, who had played Dr. Watson in a Sherlock Holmes series on television. Medium height, rather stocky, pepper-and-salt hair, a lined face—worry lines, but lots of laugh lines, too. The sort of man one trusts at sight.

"Mrs. Wren! I'm delighted to meet you." He stood, came around the desk, and shook my hand warmly. "I hope you've quite recovered from your health problems?"

I must have looked blank for a moment, until I remembered what my health problems were supposed to be. "Thank you, I'm feeling fine, just a little tired."

"Splendid! Evelyn tells me you're not only intelligent and competent, but a lover of thrillers as well. We should get on beautifully; I'm a devoted fan of the James Bond books."

"I enjoy them, too, though my great love is the detective story."

"'The normal recreation of noble minds.' Philip Guedalla, English historian and biographer; do you know him?"

"No, but I know the line. I've always agreed with it, of course!"

We talked for a few minutes, discovering also a mutual interest in flowers and gardening, before I was dismissed so courteously I hardly realized I'd been shown the door.

"Mrs. Forbes, he's everything you said he was!" I said warmly, the moment we were alone in her office. "Not only a mystery lover but a gardener as well. A remarkable man!"

She nodded somewhat complacently. "He brings the loveliest roses to the office sometimes. The perfect boss, I always say. His only fault is that he works so hard, he makes the rest of us feel guilty, and of course some of the slackers resent it. I hope you don't mind that I told him and the rest of the staff about your cancer. I thought they might be curious and ask awkward questions otherwise. Some of them aren't too tactful, I'm afraid, and it is a very wiggy-looking wig, you know, dear."

"I'm afraid it is, but I could hardly appear in public

half bald. My hair is growing back fast, though, so I may be able to abandon it soon.''

"Good. Now, the office closes at six, dear, and it's nearly that now, so be off with you, and I'll se you at nine tomorrow.''

I tidied my desk and gathered my things together, filing one more item in my tired mind as I did so.

Mr. Spragge spoke with an impeccable Oxford accent.

I walked around a couple of corners before I tried to hail a cab, and it took me so long to get one that I might almost as well have taken the tube. Tomorrow I would, I promised myself. Surely exercise would be good for my leg, as long as I didn't overdo it.

What I wanted more than anything was to take off my wig, but I had to stop at Victoria Station and pick up my luggage, and I knew what I'd look like without my second head of hair. Wig hair would be far, far worse than hat hair ever was. However, once I'd collected my gear and taken the short ride to Lynn's house, I pulled off the wretched thing; I couldn't stand it any longer. I must have looked truly awful, for Lynn took one look at me when she opened the door and went to pour me a drink.

"Sit," she commanded. Gratefully I sat; gratefully I availed myself of a little liquid relaxation. Lynn didn't even make me talk until I'd downed half of it.

"Another?"

"No, thanks, I'll wait till Tom comes home. If then. Actually I've probably had enough, but I did appreciate that one, thank you very much indeed. It's been quite a day.''

''Useful?''

''Not really. I found out a little about the personnel and the way the office works, but nothing interesting.''

''Well, wait till Tom gets here, and you can tell both of us at once.'' Lynn stood up and laid a hand on my arm. ''I *have* to do something about dinner; Tom'll be home in half an hour or so. I'd love your company in the kitchen, but you look as though you'd rather just sit.''

''You've got it.''

''Relax, then. Oh, by the way, there was a phone call for you this afternoon. Nigel Evans. Here's the number, and here's the phone. I'm off to do the chef act.''

Nigel, when I reached him, sounded mysterious.

''Dorothy.'' His voice was low and urgent. ''I must see you. Can I come up to London?''

''I—Nigel, I'm very busy during the day, I—''

''You're spying at Multilinks, aren't you?''

I capitulated. ''Yes, I've gotten a job there.'' There was no prevarication left in me.

''Good.'' I must be even more tired than I'd thought. Good? That made no sense. ''How did you know?''

''I went to your house to talk to you, and Jane told me you were in London. She acted peculiar about it, and I put two and two together. Dorothy, I need to—

I'd better not say on the phone. Can I come up tonight?''

"Tonight?"

"I can doss down with a friend, but I must talk to
you. If I called round about nine, would that do?"

"I don't know, Nigel—I'm absolutely dead beat,
and I can't just invite someone to Tom and Lynn's
house—"

I trailed off. Tom stood in the doorway. "Hey, D.,
our house is your house, you know that. Any friend
of yours—"

It's Nigel, I mouthed.

"Oh, good. Tell him to come, and we can have a
council of war. I'll tell Lynn." He saw the indecision
in my face and took the phone from my hand.

"Nigel, come anytime, you're welcome. Do you
know how to get here?"

I revived a little over dinner, and told Tom and
Lynn about the people I'd met. "No one stood out as
exceptional, I must say, and I didn't recognize anyone, but then they weren't all there. I pretty much
washed out a couple of people as possibilities for the
'doctor' on the train. The bookkeeper has shaky hands
and the wrong hair, and Mr. Spragge has the wrong
accent. I suppose either of them could be in cahoots
with whoever the 'doctor' was, though. The salespeople were all out doing their thing, and the assistant
director, or assistant to the director, or whatever he's
called—honcho number two—apparently works out
of the office most of the time." I stopped just short
of saying he was the one I suspected most. Just in

time, I remembered I wasn't supposed to have had any previous contact with the Multilinks people.

"Did you get a feel for how business is doing, D.? Was the office busy?"

"Tom, I've never been in a commercial business office for more than five minutes in my life, and then I was only paying a bill. Busy compared to what? There were quite a few phone calls, and the staff didn't seem to be twiddling their thumbs or playing solitaire at their desks. Oh, by the way, did you know you can play solitaire on a computer? Nigel showed me! It's fascinating; when it comes out, the cards start jumping all over the screen...." I trailed off; they both had that patient look on their faces. "I guess you knew that."

"Sign of a misspent middle age," said Tom with a grin. "But you're right, it was really neat the first time."

"Oh, all right, you two! So I'm getting into the twentieth century a little late."

"Just as it's about to become the twenty-first," Lynn put in.

I stuck my tongue out at her.

Nigel showed up a little before nine. I was unashamedly beginning to yawn; the day had started awfully early and had been awfully taxing.

"You look tired," he said by way of greeting.

"Thank you so much. Flattery always makes a woman feel so much better. I am in fact exhausted, and I don't mind admitting it. What do you have for me?"

He looked at Tom and Lynn.

"They know."

"Right." For once he didn't banter or argue. He sat down, put his chin in his hands, and told me.

"I've been asking questions here and there, trying to pick up any information that might be useful. I'll not go into just how, because it's rather circuitous, but I have learned something that you'll want to know."

He leaned a little farther in, became a little more intent. "Dorothy, you said that companies in the small countries, the developing countries, don't seem to be buying the Multilinks program. I suppose Tom told you that."

"You're right."

"And I got it from reliable business sources," said Tom.

"Well, I'm telling you that it just isn't true," said Nigel flatly.

"But—" said the three of us in unison, and Nigel put out a hand.

"No, wait for it. Tom, we have information from two different sorts of people, you and I, and my blokes contradict yours. I've been talking to students, chaps from all over the place. India, Africa, the West Indies, you name it. Oh, I've been subtle about it, you needn't worry. But I've talked to at last a couple of dozen of them over the past few days, and they all say the same thing. Every one of them knows of at least one company in his own country who's bought the software. Some of them are even aware that it's being used in government departments. And you know we looked up the sales records on the Multi-links computer, Dorothy? I looked at them again, and not a single one of these customers is listed. Not one!''

''Oh.'' I was too tired to worry about divulging our hacking activities, nearly too tired to think at all. ''Oh, Nigel, there has to be some simple explanation. I expect they could have bought the thing quite a while ago, or from the American office, or...or something.'' I waved a vague hand.

''Of course I thought of that. So I looked up the American sales records as well, for the past year. That's when the product was launched, a year ago. None of the names are there, either.''

We all sat and looked at each other. A stirring of interest began to make itself felt under my weariness. ''That's peculiar,'' I said slowly. ''I don't understand what it means, but it's peculiar.''

''Oh, I know what it means,'' said Nigel slowly. ''That is, I can guess what's happening, I just can't understand it. Someone is pirating the software, that's clear enough.''

I looked at him without comprehension, but Tom nodded soberly.

''Making their own copies and selling them at discount,'' he explained. ''It can be done. How difficult would it be with this program, Nigel?''

''With all the encryption they've built into this little beauty, it wouldn't be easy. And it's illegal as hell, with quite severe penalties. The part I can't understand is why someone who's actually a part of the company would take such a risk."

"Does it have to be someone in the company?" I asked.

Nigel looked at me pityingly. "You think one of the company officers killed Bill Monahan. The inference is obvious."

I shook my head. "I'm sorry, Nigel, nothing is obvious to me just now. My brain has shut down. What do you think I should do?"

"For tonight," Lynn said decisively, "you're not going to do anything except go to bed. Nigel, you're welcome to stay the night here, but we're not going to work out any more puzzles until morning."

"No, thanks, I've got a nice bit of floor at a friend's bed-sitter. But tomorrow, Dorothy—do you think you'll feel better tomorrow?"

I managed a short, humorless laugh. "Nigel, I'm tired, not dying. Yes, I'll be more rested tomorrow."

"Right. Do you have a key to the office?"

"Heavens, no. I'm just the receptionist, the lowliest of flunkies."

"Can you steal one?"

I was about to make an indignant retort when I remembered that I had recently encouraged him to several spots of lawlessness. "I don't know how I'd manage it," I said meekly.

"I don't think I want to hear this," murmured Tom.

"Try," Nigel insisted. "Or—could you hide in the loo until everyone has gone for the night?"

"I might hide somewhere. The bathroom is too small, only a closet, really. But why?"

"I want to have a look round that office."

"What for? Can't I look?"

"I wouldn't know what to tell you to look for. I don't know myself. Records that aren't kept on the computer, maybe. Something. Do you know enough about the business to recognize an anomaly if you saw one?"

"At the moment, Nigel, I barely recognize my own face in the mirror. An anomaly could beat me over the head, and I wouldn't notice."

"Yes, well, I could bear to make sure just what sort of funny business is going on in that company. Wouldn't you like to know yourself, since you're working in the midst of them?"

I admitted it. "So you want to do some burglary?"

"I don't think it's burglary if you don't steal anything. And it won't be breaking and entering either, if you let me in. Tomorrow night, if we can. When would be a good time, do you think?"

"I don't know. I think sometimes Mr. Spragge works pretty late. You'll have to call me, I suppose." I gave him the number. "It's perfectly safe; I answer the phone. But for goodness' sake, just in case anyone else answers, don't forget that I'm Louise Wren, not Dorothy Martin. We're crazy even to think of this, Nigel."

"You're right about that." Lynn stood, arms akimbo, ready to drag me up the stairs.

"You got me into it in the first place," Nigel pointed out.

"And I regret it bitterly. Go away, Nigel. I need my sleep. Call me tomorrow afternoon."

I trudged up the stairs to my room. All of Multi-links could have invaded the house that night with murder on their minds; I wouldn't have heard them, or cared if I had.

TWELVE

I MET THE REST of the sales staff the next day. Mr. Upton had them all in for a meeting in the morning, and Mrs. Forbes painstakingly introduced them as they trooped into the office.

It turned out to be a very interesting gathering. After they'd been closeted for a few minutes, I understood exactly what Mrs. Forbes had meant about tempers being high. Whatever they were talking about in Upton's office, the sparks were flying so briskly that I could hear angry voices through two good, thick closed doors. When I had occasion to go into the office proper, I saw Mrs. Forbes knock on the door and ask them all to be a little more quiet, as Mr. Spragge was entertaining a potential customer.

The meeting lasted most of the morning. Try as I might, between answering phone calls and gingerly typing a couple of memos on my computer, I could hear nothing more than an angry rumble until the meeting broke up and the three salespeople erupted into the hall where I sat.

Mr. Dalal was sweating profusely through his thin suit. He looked as though his narrow, rather light brown shoes were pinching, and his voice rang out high and somewhat piercing.

"I will not take the blame! It is not my fault! I

have worked extremely hard, and I cannot be held accountable if the company insists upon pricing the product so high that small countries—''

"Oh, stuff it, Chandra!" Mrs. Shore looked sullen. Her spike heels clicked on the black-and-white marble floor. "Nobody's blaming you any more than anyone else. Our Brian's got the wind up, that's all. I don't know why he expects us to be miracle workers. The bloody thing's gone stale for some reason. Summer slump, probably. Business will pick up when this damned heat breaks. There's no reason to panic and talk about reducing the price!"

"It is easy for you to talk," whined Mr. Dalal. "You have a husband to support you. I am engaged to be married, and if I lose my job, my fiancée—" He raised his hands to the sky, showing well-worn shirt cuffs.

"Dalal, if you mention your fiancée once more, I may throw up. You are absolutely obsessed by that girl. Well, you'll find out soon enough that marriage is not necessarily love's young dream. Won't he, my sweet?" Mr. Pierce shot his own impeccable cuffs and gave Mrs. Shore a look that has meant the same thing to men and women for as long as there have been men and women.

She pushed back her abundant auburn hair with a perfectly manicured hand and returned the look.

My, my! The sparks in the sales conference were not the only ones flying around the office, it seemed. As the three quarreled their way out the door, I reflected that I understood exactly what Mrs. Forbes had meant about Vicki Shore. She was, as a school principal of mine used to say, the kind of woman who gets herself talked about. And most of the talk, my catty mind added, is probably true.

My mind also noted that Mr. Pierce had, in addition to the longest eyelashes I'd ever seen on a man, a marked Canadian accent.

The only other notable event of the morning was a little encounter between Mr. Upton and Mr. Spragge. I didn't catch the beginning of it, but as I was coming back from the bathroom, Mr. Upton came out of Mr. Spragge's office, looking extremely angry. He stood for a moment with the door open, and Mr. Spragge's voice floated out. It was pitched low, but the diction was so steely sharp that I had no trouble hearing what he said.

"You will do, Mr. Upton, what I tell you to do. I will have no further argument!"

I was shaken. Was that the genial rose grower talking?

MRS. FORBES AND I went out to lunch together again. "Do you know," she said, "I believe in formality in the office, but when we're out of uniform, so to speak, I do wish you'd call me Evelyn. I feel I've known you for such a long time."

"And please," I said promptly, "call me—" I stopped abruptly and had a coughing fit. What on earth was my assumed name?

"Are you all right?" she said anxiously. "You're not choking, are you, Louise? It is Louise, isn't it?"

"Yes, I'm fine, thank you." I could attribute my red face to the coughing. "Something went down the wrong way. And it is Louise. I narrowly escaped Louisa; my mother liked Alcott, but my father intervened."

So we got past that little awkwardness. But I began to wonder if I really was too old to play detective. I was willing to bet that when Sherlock Holmes was in disguise, he never forgot his alias!

"What did you think of the sales staff?" she asked as we walked back to the office, slowly because of the stifling midday heat. Clouds were gathering, and there was a heavy feel to the air. Our brief spell of fine weather was about to end.

"They get excited, don't they?"

"My dear! Hammer and tongs, I do assure you. Of course I could hear them quite clearly, and so could Mr. Spragge and his client. Really, Mr. Upton should be more temperate in his speech!"

"I suppose he's worried about sales figures."

"What do you mean?" Her voice was sharp. Too late, I remembered that I wasn't supposed to know about sales figures.

"Oh, I heard the three of them talking as they came out of the meeting. I inferred that sales hadn't been too good lately."

"I see." Evelyn frowned. "I hope they stopped talking about it when they left the office."

"I'm sorry to say I don't think they did. I know they were arguing about it when they went out the door."

She pursed her lips. "They must learn to be more discreet. I will mention something to Mr. Spragge. It's no good talking to Mr. Upton, especially about that— about Mrs. Shore. She has all the men in the place under her spell."

"You must admit she's an extremely beautiful woman."

"That's as may be. Handsome is as handsome does, is what my mother said, and it's what I say. Just look at the clothes she wears, will you! Skirts so short I don't know where to look. I hate to have to think it, but that woman is no lady."

Should I agree with her, or was I too new, too junior? I took the plunge. "It did seem as though there was something between her and Mr. Pierce. Or am I imagining things?"

Evelyn snorted again. "Perfectly shameless, they are! And her with a perfectly nice husband, and him with a sweet little wife!"

"Why don't they just get divorces and marry each other, if they're so smitten?"

"Oh, that Mr. Pierce is just looking for a good time, believe you me! If his wife doesn't keep him from doing that, why ruin a perfectly good arrangement? And as for her, she'd not want to leave all that lovely money, would she?"

Goodness, women can be cats when they want to be! I wouldn't have thought Mrs. Forbes could be so spiteful.

"To tell you the truth, I've had half a mind to tell Mr. Spragge what's going on, though whether he'd believe me, I don't know. He won't have that kind of thing in the office, you know. A churchwarden, Mr. Spragge is, and he doesn't approve of carryings-on, but he has too nice a mind to see a thing, even when it's right under his nose."

Well, that was fortunate for me, if true. The kind of intrigue I was carrying on right under his nose wasn't exactly the sort to which Evelyn referred, but I doubted he'd be pleased if he knew. And I'd had a little taste this morning of what he could be like when displeased.

As luck would have it, I was away from my desk for a few minutes when Mr. Fortier came in. I had been poking around a little, hoping to find a place to hide that evening if I couldn't manage to pilfer a key, and I came through the main office just as a back was disappearing through Mr. Spragge's door.

"Client?" I asked. "I'm sorry I wasn't there to announce him; I had to go to the bathroom for a minute."

"The lavatory, dear, or the loo. A bathroom is where one has a bath. No, that was Mr. Fortier. I mustn't interrupt them, but you can meet him when he leaves."

I turned away; I couldn't let Evelyn Forbes see that I was shaking. Now that the moment had come, I was terrified.

Did I really need to meet Fortier? He was the prime candidate for first murderer. I'd met all the rest of the men and failed to recognize them. Of course, I might not have anyway—but then there was his reaction on the phone that night. At the very least, he knew something. If he was the murderer, he knew me, or at least he had seen me. In any case, I hadn't come to the Multilinks office principally to identify a person. I'd come to find out what was going on, to discover a motive; and perhaps tonight Nigel and I would come up with something. Wouldn't my time be better spent working out a plan, rather than confronting a killer?

You're scared, an inner voice jeered.

Well, all right, I was. And rightly so. If Fortier recognized me, it was all over. At the very least I'd have to get out of there fast and lose the opportunity to learn anything more. At the worst...

Pull yourself together, the voice demanded. *You have to know for certain. And you know he's extremely unlikely to recognize you. You didn't recognize your own sister once, in a long red wig. He won't have the slightest idea. If it is him. And if it isn't, you've already met and talked to the murderer. So it may well be too late.*

That was not a comforting thought. I tried to distract myself by comparing the back view I had just seen with the front view that was all I'd gotten on the train. It was a pity I'd had no chance to see the train "doctor" from the rear. Backs are very distinctive, especially when combined with a gait. But I'd never seen my doctor walking.

The build was about right, I supposed. But men, unless they're extraordinarily fat or thin or tall or short, tend to look very much alike in a business suit. Fortier had a rather soft look about him, and I didn't remember that about the train man, but he hadn't been wearing a raincoat, as Fortier was today. And the train man had worn a hat. Fortier's hair looked pretty thin—but a hat disguises a lot. I'd had a friend at home who had only a fringe of hair above his ears, but in the warm hat he wore in winter, you couldn't tell he didn't have a full head of hair.

More and more I was beginning to understand why policemen are wary of eyewitness identifications. It isn't a bit easy to spot someone you've seen only for moments under conditions of stress. I had to have a better look, and really listen to Fortier talk.

I spent an anxious hour watching, between phone calls, waiting for the office door to open. The rain had begun, the sort we would have called a gully-washer back home, with distant thunder that tightened my nerves still further. I was also dithering about what to tell Nigel when he called.

There seemed to be no way that I could obtain a key to any of the office doors, either the outer door to the building or any of the inner doors. If I could hide—and there was a roomy broom closet that would do for that—I could let Nigel in through the front door easily enough; it had a spring lock that opened without a key from the inside. The office doors were another matter. In my little snooping tour I'd noticed that they had simple locks of the push-button variety—push one button in the edge of the door, and it's locked, push the other, and it's open—but yesterday I had seen Evelyn try the doors carefully before leaving. She was observant and conscientious. There was no way I could manipulate those locks without her noticing and correcting the matter.

At that point in my speculations I heard male voices in the outer office. I picked up the telephone and became engrossed in conversation with the fictitious person at the other end of the line just as Fortier came into the hallway with Mr. Spragge. They were intent on their conversation and didn't notice me particularly, but Evelyn, right behind them, put a hand on Fortier's arm, obviously wishing to introduce me. I smiled and shrugged, pointing to the phone wedged between my shoulder and my chin. "No, I'm sorry, I don't believe you have the right—no, this is Multilinks, no Multitronics—no, they're not the same. Sir, I—sir, if you'll let me explain—yes, certainly we are a software company, but we don't make computer games—"

The two men nodded absently at me, opened their umbrellas, and swept on out the front door, still talking in an undertone, Fortier nodding earnestly at every remark Mr. Spragge made. The dangerous moment was past, and I could hang up on the nonexistent wrong number. My hand was wet on the receiver.

"What a pity," said Evelyn serenely. "We don't see Mr. Fortier often, so you may have missed your chance for a week or two. How infuriating that you should have a nuisance call just then."

"Yes, isn't it?" My voice hardly trembled at all. The encounter was over, and I still wasn't sure whether or not I had just watched a murderer pass by. My little ruse had been a poor idea, really; it had prevented my hearing anything useful of Fortier's voice, and though I'd kept my face hidden, I had at the same time blocked my clear view of *his* face.

Cowardice creates terrible limitations for the amateur detective.

"Mr. Spragge won't be back this afternoon, in case you get any calls for him." Evelyn interrupted my thoughts. "You're not likely to, of course, with only half an hour till closing time."

I looked at my watch. It was four-thirty. "But—"

"Oh, did I forget to tell you? We close the office at five on Fridays. Mr. Spragge is very understanding about people wanting to get home and begin their weekend, and six o'clock traffic in London is simply frightful on a Friday."

Here, unexpectedly, was my opportunity. I seized it.

"Oh, dear," I said, trying to sound upset. It wasn't difficult; I was still shaking. "I don't quite know what I'm going to do, in that case. A friend is picking me up after work, and I told her to come at six. We're having an early meal and then going to see *Cats*. I could wait outside, I suppose, but for an hour, in the rain…"

Evelyn frowned. "Can't you ring her up?"

"She's shopping." What a good thing I'd made her a woman; shopping is always a believable female activity.

"Well, then, I suppose you'll have to wait here."

She wasn't being very gracious about it, but I went on anyway. Nothing ventured…

"Thank you, Mrs. Forbes. I can use the time to get caught up on this filing; I've been so busy I've fallen behind. And—well, I do hate to ask, but—I haven't been feeling too well this afternoon. I think those prawns at lunch might not have been good. Do you think you could leave the office door unlocked, so I could get to the bathroom—the loo, I mean—if I have to? I'll lock it when I leave, of course."

If I'd been younger, I think she might have said no, but I was in her age bracket and a dependable type. Besides, it was the kind of request that was hard for anyone with a spark of humanity to deny, and she was, after all, the one who had failed to tell me about the Friday office hours.

She bit her lip, and I waited anxiously.

"Very well. Just this once, mind. It's my responsibility to make sure everything is locked up, and I'd be called on the carpet if it wasn't."

"You can trust me. I'll be very careful."

She smiled and seemed to relax. "I'm sure you will. Actually it'll be a bit of a blessing for me. If you're to do the locking up, I can leave a trifle early myself. My daughter and grandson are coming for a little visit, and the flat needs a wash and a brushup before I meet them at Euston."

"Oh, my, there's never quite enough time to get ready for company, is there?"

"There never seems to be. Well, enjoy your evening. You'll like *Cats;* I've seen it twice. Oh, and you'd best remind Mr. Grey and Mr. Upton to lock their doors. I'll mention it, myself, but they often forget.''

''I'll check their doors myself before I leave.'' I certainly would.

Brian Upton was out the door thirty seconds after Evelyn left, and Terry Hammond shortly after that. ''What, the gorgon gone and you still here, Mrs. Wren?'' said Terry as he passed my desk.

''I'm waiting for someone. I didn't know about Friday hours. Do you really find her a gorgon? I think she's pleasant.''

''Only if you toe the mark like a good child. She rules with an iron hand, believe me. Reminds me of an old-style nanny. The only one who isn't afraid of her is old Spragge, and I wonder sometimes about him. He's always sweet as honey when she's around. Well, ta-ta! Hope your date doesn't keep you waiting!''

''It's a woman friend,'' I said, but the door had closed behind him.

That left only Mr. Grey, but before I could check on him, the phone rang.

''Multilinks International.''

''Um—Louise Wren, please.''

''Hello, Nigel,'' I said in a low tone. ''The coast is clear, or nearly. We've gotten lucky.'' I explained the situation. ''If you'll hang on a minute, I'll find out when Mr. Grey is leaving.''

He was working at his computer when I tapped on his open door. ''I'm sorry, Mr. Grey, but as I'll be here until six, I thought I'd ask if you want any calls put through to you after five.''

"Oh. No, I'm leaving in a moment, I just want to…'' He was absorbed again. I stopped at the marketing director's door just to make sure he'd forgotten to lock it before reporting back to Nigel.

"Well, he *says* he's leaving any minute, but he's pretty wrapped up in what he's doing. Everyone else is gone, though, and I've been able to arrange for some unlocked doors.''

"I hope you weren't obvious about it!''

"I hope so, too. Nigel, give me credit for a little sense, will you? Not always a lot, maybe, but a little, now and then. Mrs. Forbes accepted my explanation, and nobody else cares.

"Now, listen. I think you'd better wait until about eight or so, just to make sure everyone is well out of the way. Oh, and bring a flashlight—a torch, I mean. It'll still be daylight then, but if it keeps on raining, it'll be pretty gloomy in here, and we shouldn't turn on the lights.''

"What will you do, meanwhile?''

"There's a very nice couch in the main office. I intend to lock myself in, as soon as Mr. Grey goes, and take a nap. I'm exhausted. There's a doorbell; ring three times when you come.''

"What about your dinner?''

"I have a candy bar in my purse. I'll see you later, Nigel.''

"Eight o'clock, sharp.''

He hung up, and I busied myself with filing. All of

my files were in the hallway, so none of the work took me legitimately into the main office. I managed several trips to Evelyn's files, anyway, partly to snoop a little and see how her office was organized, and partly to keep an eye on Mr. Grey.

It was nearly six, and I was beginning to get nervous, when he finally finished whatever it was he'd been doing and shut down his computer. I was sitting at my own desk, demurely powdering my nose, when he came through.

"Ah, Mrs.—er. Still here? I thought you left some time ago."

"I'm waiting for a friend. I'm leaving soon. Have a nice weekend, Mr. Grey."

I counted to twenty after he closed the front door behind him, and then checked his office door. Not only had he forgotten to lock it, it was standing wide open with the light on. Absentmindedness is an underrated virtue.

It is also, I reflected, not usually the hallmark of a criminal. At any rate, not of a successful one.

The first thing I did when I was alone was to call the Andersons.

"Lynn, I'm terribly sorry, but I'm going to be home late. I couldn't let you know before; Nigel and I didn't work things out until about an hour ago, and then I didn't dare call you until the last person left the office. He's coming over at eight, and goodness knows how long it'll take us to find anything. If we *can* find anything. I hope you hadn't planned anything elaborate for dinner."

She laughed. "No, I knew your plans were—flexible, shall we say? We're eating out. There's a new Indian place we've been *dying* to try."

"Meanie. You know I love Indian food. I'll be thinking about you gorging yourselves on curry while I dine on a Milky Way. Look, I'm really not at all sure when I might be able to get there. Should I plan to put up at a hotel for the night? I don't want to—"

"Don't worry about it. We'll probably be up till midnight at *least,* and if you're later than that, I'll put the key under the third geranium in the right-hand window box. Have fun, and don't get into any unnecessary trouble."

At six o'clock precisely I locked the beautiful, paneled front door of the building, which had begun life as an elegant Georgian house. Fortunately, Multilinks was at present the only tenant; the three upper stories were vacant, so I was the lone occupant. I turned out all the lights just in case anybody was interested in whether I was still there, went into the main office, and settled down on the couch for my lonely vigil.

The rain showed no signs of letting up. It was no longer pouring down, and the wind and thunder had gone, but a steady, depressing drizzle had settled in, the sort that London specializes in. The traffic noises that came through the open windows were all wet noises. One of the rain gutters on the building was evidently clogged, for I could hear a loud, rapid drip-drip-drip somewhere just outside one of the windows. It annoyed me, and I found it hard to sit still.

Would it hurt anything if I did some exploring on

my own while waiting for Nigel? The house was dim, late on a rainy afternoon, but this was June. It wasn't really dark. I could easily see.

The floor plan of the house had originally been very simple. A single-fronted house (that is, one with the front door and staircase to one side, rather than in the middle) of generous proportions, it had been planned with a gracious front hall, very possibly a curved staircase, and two large rooms on the entrance floor, one facing the quiet street, one the back garden—probably drawing room and library. Fireplaces giving on a single central chimney had warmed both rooms, which were connected by two doors, one on either side of the fireplace.

The intervening years, however, had brought ill fortune to the house. Like so very many London houses, it was eventually sold to business concerns, and in the twentieth century (I was guessing) the house had been converted entirely to commercial interests. The large front hall had been partitioned into a narrow entryway leading to a steep, narrow stair. The other half of the hall, on the main floor, anyway had been converted into a kind of anteroom, at the back of which sat the receptionist's (now my) desk and filing cabinets. The front room was now three small rooms, with Evelyn's desk in the outer office and Mr. Grey and Mr. Upton holding forth in the two cubicles, which had a connecting door. A small corridor parallel to the original wall extended to a minute bathroom—loo, lavatory, call it what you will—adjacent to the door to Mr. Spragge's office, a still-attractive room that occupied half the original library and had retained its lovely paneling, though not, sadly, its fireplace. The other half of the back room was again divided in two: Mr. Hammond's windowless and rather airless hole opening off, and really a wing of, the main office, and opening off that in turn, the office nominally occupied by Mr. Fortier. Since he was virtually never in it, however, it was actually used as a catchall office/file room by the three salespeople.

This was the labyrinth Nigel and I proposed to explore when it would be a good deal darker, and by flashlight. The prospect was daunting.

I might as well leave Mr. Hammond until Nigel got there. With no windows, his room was the darkest of the lot, though some light entered from the big front window of the outer office. Very well. That left four other offices, five if one counted Evelyn's domain. Where to start?

Do the easy part first. Mr. Grey's office was small and contained virtually nothing but his desk, his computer, and a couple of chairs for customers. Furthermore it had a big window, curtained only by white nylon. I thought about closing it. I ought to, of course. All the windows ought to have been closed before I turned out the lights, so the place would look buttoned up for the weekend. But there was so little air stirring, and it was so warm inside, I felt I just couldn't. No one would see me through the curtains.

Of course, I didn't know what I was looking for, which hampered my search considerably. There was no point in my even turning on the computer. That was Nigel's area of expertise; it would wait until he was here. I was looking, I told myself, for something, anything, that would point to questionable activities.

I almost decided at that point to skip Mr. Grey. I have a lively imagination, but even I could not conceive of that anonymous little man getting up to nefarious deeds. He was just so drab, so colorless, so *nothing.*

And what better mask to hide behind? said one of the busy voices in my head. *There is no better disguise than invisibility.*

Well, Peter Grey was the most invisible man I'd ever met, but the inner voice had a point, and the man was, after all, a Canadian. I searched his desk.

He was also the neatest man I'd ever encountered. A place for everything, and everything in its place. Four pencils sharpened to the same length. Three ballpoint pens, black. A drawer full of sticky-note pads, arranged by size and color. A drawer full of computer-generated orders, arranged by date, most recent on top. Those aroused my interest at first, but I leafed through them and found no customers outside the European Community, few in fact outside England.

There wasn't even any eraser dust in his drawers. No dried-up candy, no chewing gum. Nothing.

The thought of candy, I realized, was prompted by my own hunger. I sat down in Peter's chair and bent over to rummage through my purse, which I had set on the floor.

There was a small noise outside, and the curtains

at the window stirred. I could see nothing in my hunched-up position, but I froze, not daring to move a muscle, not even breathing. A touch of breeze at last, or—something else?

THIRTEEN

Time is relative. I stayed in that hunched-over position for a thousand years, too scared to breathe deeply, but only a minute or two had elapsed on the clock before my cramped, screaming muscles had to move. I had heard nothing more, seen no further movement. Slowly, slowly, I raised my head, a millimeter at a time. The creaking of my bones sounded so loud in my ears, I was sure it could be heard in the street.

When at last I dared slew my eyes around to the window, I took one look and then sat up abruptly straight, bumping my head on the bottom of Mr. Grey's computer desk. I was limp with relief.

"Well, sir, or madam as the case may be, I hope you know you scared me out of at least three or four of *my* lives, and I don't have as many to spare as you do."

"Mrrrp," responded my visitor briefly, in a raspy soprano. It was a sorry specimen, its once-white fur damp and matted, one ear torn, one eye swollen shut. Its ribs showed, and the tip of its tail was missing. It sat on the wide windowsill and studied me for a moment and then, finding me of no interest, licked a paw and began to wash its face.

I sat back in the chair. "Now what am I going to

do with you? Poor thing, I wish I could feed you, but there's nothing you'd like here. You also need a bath, and some love, and a visit to the vet, and I can't provide any of those things right now. In fact, puss, I have things to do, and one of them is to shut this window. Could I persuade you to continue your ablutions elsewhere?''

I made a move toward the cat. It swore at me, neatly avoided my reaching hands, and jumped back down into the street. I'd learned my lesson; I closed that window and then made a tour of the office, closing them all. Better to swelter than to risk any more such heart-stopping surprises.

I now needed that candy bar I'd started to hunt for back in that other lifetime, needed it badly. When adrenaline dissipates, it leaves me starved. I pawed through my purse, found the candy, ate it, wished I had another, and sat down on the couch in the main office to think what to do next.

Whoever my ''doctor'' had been, he had certainly been working with somebody. Presumably that somebody was as deep into the pirating operation as the spurious doctor. Now who was the most likely person in the organization to be stealing the product?

Why, as Nigel had wondered, would anyone take the risk of stealing it at all? Oh, for money, of course—but when people turn to crime, it's usually for a pressing reason. They need money very badly for some special purpose—big debts, especially gambling debts, or big expenses ahead. Given the kind of fiction I prefer, my mind of course leaped to blackmail.

Who had a guilty secret?

I thought about them all.

Fortier, for a start, as the most likely person. I knew scarcely anything about him, really. He was rather young to hold an important executive post, which probably meant he was both intelligent and ambitious, as Mrs. Forbes had told me. It also seemed he was eager to cultivate the boss; I remembered those obsequious little nods punctuating his conversation with Mr. Spragge. Ambitious toadies can be dangerous people.

However, the description was unfair. I was basing it more on what I'd been told than on my own observation. No, the only real strike against Fortier was that he'd been scared when Nigel mentioned Bill Monahan on the phone. What did that mean? Was he a man with a secret? I didn't know enough yet to make a reasonable guess, so I passed on to the next candidate.

That would have to be Brian Upton, he of the violent temper, who was having some sort of quarrel with the boss. It didn't take too much imagination to come up with a secret he might be hiding. There could easily be some trouble lurking in his background, given that violent personality, and Mr. Spragge the churchwarden wouldn't like trouble. Certainly he didn't like something that Mr. Upton had been doing, or not doing, lately. I wished I'd overheard more of their little contretemps.

Definitely he wouldn't like the affair that Vicki Shore and Lloyd Pierce were carrying on with so little effort at concealment. Did Spragge really not know about it? How could he not, if he had eyes? Unless they were such valuable employees that he preferred to close his eyes to what he didn't want to see. That seemed unlikely, with the sales situation at such a dismal pitch, and it certainly didn't square with the touch of tyranny I'd observed in his personality this morning.

Chandra Dalal. He ought to be able to sell the software to his own countrymen, but apparently he couldn't. Did that mean he was selling it on his own and pocketing the proceeds? He didn't look prosperous, though, and he seemed worried about his job. Of course, he did need extra money badly, with a wedding in the offing.

Pierce and Shore dressed very well, and very expensively, but then they both had working spouses.

That was the sales staff, except for the Grey nonentity, whom I dismissed for the moment. It was of course possible that he was hiding something under that bland exterior, but if so, he was hiding it beyond my ability to penetrate the screen. Nigel might be able to find out something.

Onward. Offhand, Terry Hammond seemed one of the least likely candidates—open, a bit brash, likable, neither especially affluent nor especially impoverished in appearance. But he had a drinking problem. That was another weakness the estimable Mr. Spragge might well frown on, especially if it interfered with

Mr. Hammond's work. If he was the pirate, could he be drinking up all the extra profits? Surely not. He'd be in a perpetual coma. And he certainly didn't act like a man with a guilty secret.

I leaned back, tired. Obviously I needed to search Fortier's office. I needed to search everybody's office, and leave the computers to Nigel. And I would, as soon as I got a little energy back.

SOMETHING WAS BUZZING. An alarm clock? But why was it going on and off like that?

I sat up, trying to rub out the crick in my neck and understand why, if the alarm was ringing, there was so little light.

Silence. Then the buzzing again. Three times.

Oh, Lord, *Nigel!*

I banged my knee into some obstacle and my elbow into another as I ran for the door.

"I thought you weren't coming!" he said in a furious whisper. "I thought something had happened to you! And you don't even look like you. My God, never do that to me again!"

"I'm not likely to!" I snapped. My knee and my elbow hurt, not to mention my neck and my back and virtually everything else about my person. We stood glaring at each other in the hallway.

I recovered first. "All right, Nigel, I'm sorry. I was asleep when you rang the bell, and I couldn't seem to wake up properly, and then I kept running into things. I'm going to have bruises tomorrow. The wig—well—the wig is supposed to be a disguise. I'm sorry you were worried.''

"I wasn't worried, I was bloody scared! There's a copper just round the corner!''

Nigel almost never swears around me. He must be in a real state. "All right, love, you didn't get caught, and I said I'm sorry. Did you bring the flashlight?''

"Yes, but it's only a small one. I didn't think we'd better risk a big torch.''

"And how right you are, with windows all over the place and only thin nylon curtains. We're going to have to be careful.''

We went into my inner hall, which had a little light coming from the window and the back door. Nigel shone his torch around, cautiously, and then sat down on the visitors' bench.

"Okay, what's the drill?''

"I hope you'll tell me. I haven't discovered a thing.'' I settled in my own chair, rubbing my elbow, and explained about my abortive efforts earlier. "The only evidence I could come up with was negative, I'm afraid. There was nothing in Mr. Grey's desk of any conceivable interest. And then I panicked at the stupid cat and ate my stupid candy bar, and then I fell asleep. Not a good showing at all, I'm afraid.''

"That reminds me,'' said Nigel. He reached into the backpack he always wore. "For you. My mate's local does good bar food.'' The sandwich was somewhat squashed, but it smelled of good bread and roast beef and horseradish. My mouth began to water, and my stomach made eager little growls. "You are a lifesaver, my dear. Would you like to share?"

"No. I've eaten, and there's another if I get hungry later. Feel free."

While I ate ravenously, he lectured.

"My basic idea is this. Our pirate is a businessman, and there are large sums of money involved, so he'll keep records of what he's doing. Obviously he's not likely to keep them on the company computer. Well, you'd have to be daft to put them where just anyone could access them, wouldn't you? Bu this is a computer age, and these are computer people. They won't keep the records on paper, either, I'm betting."

"So what's left?"

"A personal computer, not connected to the company network. If it's a desktop in someone's house, we're out of luck. But if it's a laptop, there's just the bare chance it might be here somewhere. Did you see everyone leave today?"

I thought about that. "Yes."

"Did they take briefcases?"

"I don't think—I'm not sure, but I don't think any of them did."

"Then we have a chance. I brought a bottle of Bass, too. Sorry, but you'll have to drink it warm, the proper English way."

"The proper English way," I retorted, "is to serve beer at cellar temperature, and if you've been carrying that thing around next to your back, it'll be a lot warmer than a cellar. I'll pass for right now, thank you. You can have it."

"There are two. Later, when we've finished?"

"Good idea."

"Right. On our bikes, then."

It would have been more efficient to divide the search, but with only one flashlight we had to work together. We started in my cubbyhole. A laptop computer can be hidden almost anywhere, and I hadn't been through all my filing cabinets yet.

We found nothing. No electronic gadgets, no software or data disks, nothing but memos, phone messages, old files, and the paper that somehow or other clutters up even the most resolutely "paperless" office.

On to the main office and Evelyn's files. Nothing peculiar. Some crochet patterns tucked away; a small stash of paperback thrillers and a collection of Sayers short stories in a file drawer; some pictures, probably of her grandchildren.

I'd already declared Peter Grey a washout, and Nigel, after a quick search through his computer, came to the same conclusion. In Brian Upton's office, we did find some interesting things.

We had gone through his desk drawers rapidly, looking for a computer. I tried to shut the top drawer, but it was messy, crammed full of junk, and the top piece of paper caught on something and didn't want to lie down. I picked it up to smooth it and replace it the way it was.

"Nigel, shine the light over here."

"Something?"

"I'm not sure. Can you read it? I think I can make

out a little, but English handwriting isn't my strong point.''

''Whew! What a beastly scrawl! I'm not sure if I can decipher it out, but let's see—oh, dear, dear, dear!''

''Then it's what I thought it was?''

Nigel read it aloud. '''If you think'—there's no salutation, just starts off—'If you think I shall peg'—no—'pay a—a filthy blackmailer'—actually, it doesn't say 'filthy,' but that's the idea—''

I smiled. ''Go on.''

'''—pay a filthy blackmailer a thousand pounds or any other bleeding'—sorry—'amount, you can go straight to hell and'—'' Nigel stopped abruptly and cleared his throat. ''Well, it suggests what the blackmailer might do on his way to his destination. And that's the end of it.''

My smile broadened. Nigel really could be a love. ''My dear boy, I've probably heard the words before. Not that I had any desire to hear them again, so thank you. Well!''

''Blackmail. What about? Is he our pirate?''

''He certainly could be. Except—would he draft a reply, in that case? This must be a draft, since he obviously hasn't sent it, and it sounds to me like 'Publish and be damned.' He would only take that attitude for one of two reasons. Either he truly doesn't care if whatever it is comes out, which doesn't sound like high-end piracy, or he plans to dispatch the blackmailer, in which case he wouldn't write to him in these terms and leave the first draft lying around. Does that make sense?''

"Mmm." Nigel, who had sounded excited, now sounded deflated. "I suppose so. Let's look through the drawers again."

This time the back of a bottom drawer yielded overlooked treasure. Two plastic bags were stuffed inside a manila envelope.

"That's cannabis," said Nigel without hesitation, pointing to one bag. "And that looks very much like crack cocaine."

I didn't question how Nigel knew, but I thought it was probably through friends, rather than personally, especially in the case of the crack. Nigel drinks a bit more than he should at times, but since he has married, at least, he's been a pretty responsible citizen overall. My concern at the moment was more immediate. "Oh, my word, Nigel, and our fingerprints are on them!"

"Not to worry." He pulled a wrinkled, but clean, handkerchief from a pocket and wiped the surfaces of both bags and, as best he could, the envelope. "Not that anyone is likely to look, but we might as well be careful."

I wondered what Alan would say if he knew I had just handled controlled substances and then watched while evidence was destroyed. Oh, well. Alan was far away.

"I expect we now know what he was being blackmailed about, Nigel. And at the moment I don't care by whom. Let's continue, and for heaven's sake be careful with that flashlight. We do *not* need a bobby seeing a light in here and coming to investigate.''

Mr. Spragge's door was locked. I hadn't been able to figure out any way to get Evelyn to leave it open. I'd have to try to find a way to search his office myself, though I wasn't sure how.

There was no door to Mr. Hammond's office, only the open doorway to the left of where the drawing room fireplace would have been, so we had no trouble there, and very little trouble finding the bottle of vodka in the bottom drawer, under a few papers.

"So he drinks on the job, as well," I said sadly. I rather liked Mr. Hammond, and alcoholism is one of the cruelest of the fists that can grip a man and choke the humanity out of him.

"Does he do his work properly?" Nigel wanted to know.

"As far as I know. I don't know a lot about bookkeeping, do you?"

"Not a farthing's worth. But he gets to his desk on time, that sort of thing?"

"Nigel, I've been here two days, and yesterday not till ten. How would I know Terry Hammond's attendance record? What does it matter, anyway? Except to him, poor man."

"We're looking for a reason to steal. If a man doesn't work, he's sacked. If he's sacked, he has no income. Ergo, if this chap makes a habit of getting drunk on the job and being sacked, he has money problems, and a reason to steal. *Quod erat demontrandum.*"

"All right, one for you, Nigel. But I don't know the answer."

We found nothing else of interest there, and moved on, with a shiver on my part, to Mr. Fortier's office, which was never kept locked because of the others who used it casually.

This was a back room; its window looked out on what was once probably a fine garden but was now no more than a walled patch of scrubby grass with a rosebush or two struggling for survival. The houses behind it were either vacant or occupied by businesses, and were dark at this hour of the night.

Nigel shone his light around the room briefly and whistled. "Lot of rubbish in here."

"Yes, and this is the most likely spot, Nigel. Mr. Fortier works in here, when he works at the office at all. So do the other sales staff. We need to make a thorough job of this."

"It'd take all night, I reckon. Can we risk the light, do you think, so we can work independently?"

I looked dubiously at the rectangle of window through which murky twilight filtered into the room. "I don't know. They made windows awfully big back when this place was built. Maybe if—is there a desk lamp?"

There was. I moved it to the floor near Mr. Fortier's desk, shaded it around with some file folders, and crouched there, examining the contents of one drawer at a time while Nigel shone his torch over the apparently random piles of papers that occupied every desk surface and a good part of the floor.

Time passed. We searched, growing more and more discouraged. At last I tottered to my feet with loud groans. "Nothing. How about you?"

"No laptop computer, at least. Most of the papers I've seen are forms of one sort or another, and dull as ditchwater."

We looked at each other despairingly in the dim light. "Nigel, this is infuriating! I'm really very suspicious of Mr. Fortier, but this place is such a rat's nest, anything could be hidden here, and we'd never find it!"

Nigel nodded soberly. "I'm not sure there's a point to looking further."

"There's still Mr. Spragge's office." I sighed as I said it. I was very tired and getting very discouraged.

"But it's locked."

"Yes, well, I thought you might—"

"Pick a lock? Not a chance! Do you know, for such a respectable, honest-looking lady you are a menace to society!"

"And you are—Nigel, what's that over there? Let me have the light for a second."

I shone it against the wall, and there, sure enough, in the modern partition dividing this office from Mr. Spragge's, a door had been cut, plain, inconspicuous, flush with the wall. "Aha! So the boss can confer with his second in command. If the second were ever here, anyway. And I'll bet..."

The door wasn't even made to lock. So much for security. We carefully put everything back the way we had found it and entered Mr. Spragge's office.

Seen by daylight, I knew, it was a beautiful room. The proportions had been spoiled when it was cut up, of course, but the walnut paneling still glowed softly with the patina that only proper care can maintain. The large, impressive desk was of the right period and also beautifully cared for. The boss, furthermore, had treated himself not only to a rich Persian carpet but to fine, dusty blue velvet draperies. I moved to the window and pulled them carefully shut.

"Now. Let there be light."

The rest of the office complex suffered the glare of recessed fluorescent fixtures. Here a fine brass chandelier provided softer, more gracious light. It was sufficient, however.

We found the computer almost at once, turned on its side and pushed in among the books in one of the arched, built-in bookcases.

"Eureka!" said Nigel.

"You're very classical tonight, Nigel. Is it really, though?"

"It's certainly a laptop, and it was certainly tucked away, if not exactly hidden. As to whether it's what we want…"

He had turned it on as he spoke and, once the screen responded, began to peck eagerly at the keyboard like a robin digging for worms. I leaned avidly over his shoulder.

"Wow." He said it very softly, almost with awe.

"What? I can't see, the screen is all purple."

He tilted it for me, the contrast seemed to adjust itself, and I saw.

It read like a roster of the United Nations. Every poverty-stricken nation I'd ever heard of, and quite a few I hadn't, was among the addresses scrolling up the screen. Sales dates, figures, contact names, were all there. The figures were totaled now and then to sums I found staggering.

"Mr. Spragge," I said numbly. "But why? He must earn a fortune at this job. Well, we know he does. We've seen his salary."

"Greed—" began Nigel.

"I don't believe it. He's just not that kind of man. He's a man of principle, a churchwarden."

"And how long did you say you'd been employed here?" His voice dripped with sarcasm. "You seem to know him awfully well for such short acquaintance."

"Okay, okay, but he really is! I don't say he's an angel, but you only have to take one look at him—*what was that?*"

The last words came out in a panicky squeak. We'd both heard the noise from the adjacent office.

Nigel moved to the light switch, turned it off as silently as he could, and then very slowly eased open the connecting door.

Something rubbed against my ankles and uttered a plaintive mew.

Nigel made a disgusted noise and pointed the flashlight in the direction of the mew. "Is that all? Only the office—"

"Nigel, hush! No, don't turn the lights back on!" My voice was a whisper that didn't seem to have enough breath behind it. "The office doesn't have a cat, and I shut this one out hours ago. Nigel—*how did it get in here?*"

FOURTEEN

IT TOOK NIGEL two seconds to absorb that. Then he made for the door. "We have to get out of here!"

"Yes, but where's the computer? We've got to put it back!"

We found it easily. It was still turned on, its screen glowing eerily in the darkened room. Nigel took more time than I liked to turn it off.

"Hurry!" I urged.

"I have to do this properly," he muttered. "If I just shut it down without saving the files, I could destroy the data, and they'd know someone had been at it." He finished, finally, and jammed the computer back into the bookshelf. We took a last panicky look around the room to see if it looked more or less normal and tried again to leave. The problem was the cat. Perfectly content in a dry place, on a warm, soft rug, it had begun to wash itself and purr loudly.

"Here, puss," said Nigel very quietly. "Nice puss!"

The cat, centered in the flashlight beam, dealt with a troublesome spot on its right shoulder blade.

"Stupid animal," Nigel muttered, and made a grab for it. A paw flashed out; Nigel swore and sucked his hand. The cat went on purring.

"Here, kitty, kitty," I pleaded. I could have sworn the beast rolled its eyes in disgust.

"Damn! We can't leave it here to give the game away, but if someone is still in the building, or hanging about—"

"I know. Listen, Nigel, did you say you had another sandwich?"

He rummaged in his backpack, produced the sandwich, and extracted a bit of beef. Without a glance at the cat, he put it on the floor and moved back toward the door.

The beef was gone in an instant. Nigel put down a little more, retreated a little farther....

I followed to shut the door on the cat once it was out of Mr. Spragge's office, but we still had several rooms to go before we reached the outside door. Progress was excruciatingly slow, and I began to fear that the food would run out before our feline tormentor was safely on the front step.

"This is the last of it," Nigel said when we had gotten as far as my vestibule. He put his pack on the floor, opened it, and laid the small piece of beef in the far corner.

I didn't think it would work. The cat was a wary, wily stray. It was, however, also very hungry, and the beef was obviously the best thing that had come its way for days.

Neither of us breathed. The cat, slinking low on its belly, crawled to the pack, sniffed the human smell, hesitated, and then dove to the back.

Nigel clapped the top half down, picked up the

pack, and managed, with the assistance of me and gravity, to get the zipper done up.

Unearthly yowls proceeded from inside, along with writhings and ominous scraping noises as sharp claws tried to open an escape path.

"Extra-heavy-duty nylon, I hope?"

"Industrial strength," said Nigel. "And nearly new, so the little bugger had best not shred it if he knows what's good for him. Now what?"

"Now we fade away as quietly as possible. I do wish that beast would *hush!*"

But it didn't hush until we got outside and down the steps. It was still drizzling. I put up my umbrella. "You can let it go now, Nigel," I reminded him.

Nigel put the pack down and unzipped it. The cat poked its head out, sniffed the rain, and looked at us.

Then it uttered a brief comment and curled back up in the pack.

I suppose it was reaction. Nigel and I looked at each other and began to shake with laughter. We laughed so hard, we almost fell over. "I don't suppose," I said weakly when I couldn't laugh anymore, "that there'd be a pub open anywhere. I could use a drink after that."

"I've those bottles of Bass," said Nigel, wiping his eyes.

"No, thank you. A lady doesn't drink on a park bench in the rain. Besides, we've got to move on. I don't know what we're thinking of. If anyone's still around..."

Again I didn't finished the thought, but it sobered

both of us in a hurry. Nigel shouldered the pack again, zipping it enough so that the cat would stay dry and still be able to breathe, and we headed for Russell Square, the nearest place to find a cab at that hour of the night. I refused to deal with the Underground just then.

We snared a cab right out from under the doorman at the Russell Hotel and climbed in. "Yes, sir?" said the cabbie.

He looked at Nigel, and Nigel looked at me. I shrugged. "We might as well go back to the Andersons'. They'll want to know all about it, and Lynn said they'd be up till midnight." I gave the cabbie the address, and we sat back in silence, each absorbed in our own thoughts. The silence didn't last long. The cat soon made it earsplittingly clear that it did not care for automobile travel. The cabbie turned around at the first yowl, shook his head, and firmly shut the connecting window.

The cat was still yowling at the top of its considerable lungs when we got to the house in Belgravia. I reached for the bell, but Lynn opened the door before my finger hit the button.

"I suppose you heard the cat," I said weakly.

"I imagine the *Queen* heard the cat. Buck House is only a half mile away, after all, and this is a quiet neighborhood. Ordinarily. For heaven's sake get the creature inside before my neighbors get up a petition!"

Seen against the backdrop of Lynn's exquisite period furniture, the cat looked more disreputable than ever. Once Nigel opened the backpack, it sat perfectly still for a few minutes, only its nose and ears twitching. Then, stepping delicately, it began to wander around the room, belly low to the ground and tail tucked under, exploring the new territory with every sense alert.

"All right, where did you pick up this one? And if you don't mind my saying so, why?" Tom's voice was critical, and I can't say I blamed him.

"I had nothing to do with it. Cats choose their people, you know that. I wouldn't have chosen this one, but it decided it wanted to come home with us."

"What are you going to do with it?" asked Lynn. "Emmy and Sam wouldn't like it a bit, would they?"

"Probably not. Actually I expect I'll take it back where it came from, but meanwhile you don't have any food it could eat, do you? The poor thing's half starved, even after demolishing an entire sandwich. Look at its ribs."

Tom groaned. "Feed a stray cat, and it's yours for life, you know, D."

Lynn said nothing, but slipped out to the kitchen and came back with a large saucerful of minced chicken. She also brought a plate of sandwiches for the humans, and some beer at the proper temperatures for both English and American tastes. We enjoyed our treat, but not with quite the enthusiasm of the cat, who devoured the chicken in a few bites.

"It'll soon fatten up if it goes on eating that way," said Nigel with a grin. "Or he will. I'll lay odds he's a tom, and a fighter, too. We'll have to turn him loose, I suppose. He's no pet.''

''No.'' I surveyed the cat, now licking a paw industriously. ''It seems a pity, though. The poor thing could use a little love.'' I yawned widely. ''And besides that, he's a clue, in a way.'' I explained quickly, for Tom and Lynn's benefit. ''What I want to know is how he got into the building,'' I concluded.

''Back door?'' asked Tom.

''It's kept locked. It's just beyond my desk in the hall. Evelyn explained it's a fire exit and has to be kept clear, but it's never used, and certainly never left open.''

''Are there fire stairs outside?''

''I haven't noticed, but I suppose there are. And yes, it's just conceivable that Sneaky Pete there—''

''Sneaky Pete?'' That was Nigel.

''It's another name for moonshine whiskey. Seems appropriate for a white cat that sneaks around. Anyway, he might have climbed up the outside stairs, if there are any, and gotten in through an upstairs window, though it seems most unlikely that any would have been left open in empty offices. But he didn't, I'll swear, open that door from the hall by himself. Somebody let him in, Nigel. Probably without knowing it; opened the door, and the cat slipped in. They do that.''

''When?''

''It could have been almost any time after I fell asleep. I slept for over an hour, and then you came along, and we started exploring. Would we have heard anyone?''

Nigel, dropping to a seat on the floor and nursing his beer, thought about that for a moment. ''I don't know. I think so. We weren't making a row.''

''But we were concentrating on what we were doing, and that's a solid old house. I can't be sure. But the more I think about the whole incident, the less I understand it.'' I punched the pillows on the couch into a more comfortable configuration and leaned back against them.

''Someone came into that building, either before you arrived or after. If it was before, I don't understand what he—she—they did. Where they went. They didn't come into the main office, because that's where I was asleep, and I would have known. I wasn't all that dead to the world.''

''No?'' asked Nigel, one eyebrow quirked.

''Well—all right, it took me a while to hear the doorbell. But it doesn't really sound very loud inside. And I *know* I'd have waked if someone had turned on a light, or shone a flashlight around. Light has always wakened me.''

''Mmm.'' Nigel didn't sound convinced, but I went on anyway.

''Okay, so if they came while I was asleep they either went upstairs—but why?—or just hung around. And again, why? But if they came *after* you were there—well, then, what did they do? The same thing. Nothing. I don't understand.''

"You're assuming this unknown person is connected with Multilinks?" Tom asked.

"Well, who else would it be? Come on, Tom, the skeptical attitude is fine, but anyone who would come to the office late on a Friday and skulk around has to be in on this piracy business. And in that case, you'd think they would have dispatched us on the spot."

"You read too many mysteries," said Nigel with some scorn. "People aren't that eager to do murder in this country, you know."

"They've done it once, and as the old saying goes, you can't be hanged twice. Well, not even once, since you did away with capital punishment, but the rule holds. We're dealing with a murderer, Nigel, and he probably caught us in the act of burgling his office. Why didn't he kill us?"

"You've decided it's Spragge, then? I thought you thought he was a verray parfit gentil knight."

"I didn't *say* that! I said I couldn't understand, on the basis of his character, *why* he would do such a thing. But he's a complex man, and I can't deny that you found the computer in his office."

That was something else we had to explain to Tom and Lynn. When we'd finished, Tom frowned.

"Now, there's another assumption you're making, D. You found the computer in Spragge's office, so you say it's his."

"Well—yes."

Tom sighed. "A laptop computer, D. Think about it. The principal feature of a laptop is that it is portable. And if it contains incriminating evidence, did you ever stop to consider why you found it?''

I sat up and slapped my forehead. ''Good grief, I'm getting too old for this! We were intended to find it— is that what you're saying?''

''Or someone was, at some time. Tell us about the people who work there.''

We went over the office personnel exhaustively. At the end Nigel summed them up.

''So. We have one who drinks, one who drugs and has a violent temper, probably related to the drugs. Two, both married, are having an affair. One's a washout as a salesman, and one's a washout as a person. Is that the lot?''

''And a boss and a secretary and an assistant boss who I think is a murderer.''

''But you're not certain.''

''No. If he was the man in the train, and I'm still not certain even about that, then he at least knew about the murder and disposed of the body. He couldn't have done that alone, though, and his helper, or helpers, might actually have committed the murder.''

Nigel unwound himself from his position on the floor. ''Then I move we adjourn. We're getting nowhere, it's a filthy time of night, and you've been yawning for an hour at least. If I could get on the blower and fetch a minicab, Lynn, I'll take myself back to Earl's Court and my mate's flat.''

''But it's late! Please do stay here.''

''No, there's Pete, you see.'' Nigel jerked a thumb

at the cat, now peacefully asleep on a Louis XIV chair. "I think he'd be better off where the furniture comes from Oxfam and scratches don't matter."

FIFTEEN

"ALAN CALLED last evening, before you came home," said Lynn at the breakfast table. I had slept very late. Tom had gone off early to play golf with some cronies; Lynn and I were enjoying a lazy Saturday morning. "I'm so sorry; I forgot to tell you last night, in all the excitement. It would have been too late for you to return the call, anyway."

I put down my coffee. "Oh, dear, I meant to call him no later than yesterday. I guess I'd better—what did he want?"

"Oddly enough, he wanted to talk to you," said Lynn tartly, and then she laughed. "Don't look so worried. I released *no* cats from their bags. Didn't I tell you I can lie beautifully when I have to? I was absolutely charming, said you'd be *devastated* to miss him, but you were out and I wasn't sure when you'd be back—which was the absolute *truth,* you know. As soon as he supplied the assumption that you were at some sort of prenuptial festivity, it was plain sailing, but it *would* have been somewhat easier if I'd known from the start which cover story you were using."

"You're an angel, and brilliant, and I apologize all over the place." I recited all the details I could remember of the goddaughter fairy tale, and then finished my coffee and went off to call Alan.

He sounded happy to hear from me and just a little worried. I soothed him (I hoped) with apocryphal stories about the shopping I'd done and the party Friday night.

"When did you say she's being married?"

Oh, dear heaven! Had I given him a day? What should I say? How long was it going to take me to wind things up at Multilinks? Or to decide I was wasting my time? Alan would expect me to be in Sherebury after the nonexistent wedding was over. When could I reasonably expect to go home?

"Dorothy?"

The pause had lasted far too long. "Yes, sorry, love. My earring fell off, and I was feeling around on the floor for it. It's on Wednesday afternoon. The wedding, I mean, not my earring. But I may stick around here for a day or two afterwards to have some time with Tom and Lynn. I've hardly had a chance to talk to them, I've been out so much...." I was talking nervously, saying whatever came into my head. "When do you expect to be home, yourself? You've been gone an awfully long time."

"By the end of next week, and perhaps sooner. That's why I asked you about the wedding. I'll know for certain by Wednesday at the latest. I'll phone then and let you know, or leave a message. You'll undoubtedly be out all day."

Undoubtedly. I was surprised to feel tears rush to

my eyes. "Oh, Alan, you don't know how much I've missed you!"

"I think I may have some slight idea," he said, and I could almost see the twinkle in his eye. "Have a lovely weekend, darling, if this demanding god-daughter of yours gives you any time to yourself. I'll see you soon."

Alan was coming home! I could tell him all about it and get his advice and turn the whole mess over to him. I could hardly wait.

But of course I was going to have to. Glumly I hung up the phone and moped into the living room. "I owe you a lot of money, I expect. Let me know when you get the phone bill."

"*Don't* be silly. No bad news, I hope?"

It's a good thing I don't play poker. My face hides my feelings about as well as plate glass. "No, it's just that Alan's coming home."

"And that makes you look like Jeremiah? I hadn't realized the honeymoon was over so soon."

"Now you're the silly one! I'm so anxious to see him it hurts, that's all. Somehow, talking to him made me really feel how far away he is, and how much I've needed him. Besides, I had to lie to him, and I hate that."

"My *dear!* How could you *possibly* do anything else? You can't count on *anything* being private these days. You'll tell him the *whole* story the *minute* he gets home, and he can make the idiotic police see reason. If you haven't tied the entire matter up with *ribbons* by then, of course. Now, when is that darling man going to be back where he belongs?''

"Not till the end of next week, probably. He wasn't exactly sure.''

"Very well, then, we're going to spend the rest of the weekend being normal people, doing normal things, and keeping your mind off your troubles. The weather's turned *gorgeous.* How recently have you been to Kew Gardens?''

The Royal Botanic Gardens, to give them their proper name, were once the gardens of Kew Palace, at that time (around the time of George III) a royal residence. Some of the plantings are well over two hundred years old, and in total, they represent a kind of living museum of plants, rare and beautiful, from all over the world. At any time of year Kew is worth an extended visit. On a gorgeous June day the gardens were heavenly, but of course very crowded. Lynn had had the foresight to bring a lunch, which we ate sitting in the rose garden.

I couldn't leave my problem alone, even in the midst of all that beauty.

"Mr. Spragge grows roses," I said suddenly. Lynn looked a little startled; we had been talking about poor old Queen Charlotte.

"Does he? I suppose you think that unfits him for the role of murderer.''

"I don't know what to think of him, and that's the truth. Mrs. Forbes thinks he's the paragon of all virtues. He's been charming to me. But I saw the sales manager come out of his office yesterday, and if looks could kill, believe me, we would now be dealing with the murder of Mr. Spragge.''

"Hmmm. Sounds a little like a boss Tom had once. Delightful man, cultured, warm—and *utterly* ruthless. Once he decided on a course of action, the angel Gabriel wouldn't have been able to talk him out of it, I *do* assure you.''

"Then you think Spragge—''

"I don't think anything at all. I don't know the people involved. Just watch yourself, that's all. Charm can hide a good many sins. Now you've sat *quite* long enough, and you've talked about your worries far too long. You were going to get your mind off them, remember? We're off to the Palm House, where the temperature and humidity combined will prevent your mind from working at all.''

When we had completely worn ourselves out, we left the gardens and had tea at the Maids of Honor, a wonderful old place nearby that's famous for an almond-flavored tea pastry by the same name, of which I am inordinately fond. Once Tom heard that we'd gorged ourselves, he resigned himself to leftovers for supper, after which we went to a nightclub where I was amazed to hear good jazz.

Sunday morning I went to church at St. Peter's Eaton Square, a church nearby renowned for its music and its society weddings, and in the afternoon we all three did a little mild sightseeing in Belgrave Square, a lovely park surrounded by lovely houses, many with connections to my beloved mystery fiction. Lynn and Tom between them refused to allow me to talk about

Multilinks at all, which was perhaps just as well, but I was restless, itching to get back to my problem. I wanted to have it over and done with by the time Alan showed up.

Apparently my subconscious was working the whole time, for on Monday morning I sailed off to the Underground station, in my wig and silly glasses, eager to pursue the new ideas in my head.

Someone at Multilinks had been spying on us Friday night. That much was virtually certain. But it could have been anybody, from the exalted Mr. Spragge right down to the anonymous Mr. Grey, and I had no idea who.

When I got the chance today, then, I was going to ask people about their weekends. Perfectly normal thing to do, after all, after two days of gorgeous weather. Then I might be able to piece together a picture of where the staff had been when, and perhaps identify the person I had begun in my mind to call the lurker.

Of course, the lurker would lie about Friday night, but I hadn't taught school for over forty years without getting pretty good at spotting liars. And I had one other very small advantage. I was almost sure the lurker was unaware that we knew he/she had been there. We had never seen or heard the slightest evidence of the lurker's presence, except for the cat. And I doubted the cat was a deliberate ploy. Cats will almost never do what you want them to, and this particular criminal was too smart to risk anything on a possibly uncooperative animal. No, our lurker had come in, in absolute quiet, had become aware of our presence, and had left again, not knowing the cat had been left behind as mute evidence.

So I could watch for lies, and I could also lie about my own activities and watch for a reaction without, I thought, being suspected.

I certainly hoped so, anyway. I shuddered, despite the stifling heat in the crowded Underground train. This was, I reminded myself once more, a murderer I was trying to fool.

I had to think very strenuously about poor Bill Monahan to keep from turning around and heading for home right then. About him, a young man lying dead, never to see London...and about the fact that I was already too deeply committed to get out. I had my tiger by the tail now, and there could be no letting go until its claws were clipped.

I was a little early getting to the office. Evelyn Forbes was just unlocking the door as I walked up, which made me very glad I'd taken the Underground instead of a taxi. The persona of a somewhat impoverished Louise Wren had to be maintained.

"Good morning, Evelyn! Beautiful morning, isn't it?"

"Oh, yes, indeed, glorious." She didn't sound very happy about it.

"How was your weekend with your family?"

She let me in the door and groaned. "Exhausting, actually. Sheila, that's my daughter, didn't get in until quite late on Friday, and of course I worried, because I'd expected her on the eight-seventeen, but it was delayed and she had no chance to ring me. Then she had some shopping to do on Saturday, so she left young Richard with me. All afternoon! He's a perfect love, of course, but he's four years old.''

"Oh, dear. I remember my nieces and nephews at that age. Nonstop energy.''

"And then on Sunday we went to Brighton, and it was so crowded and hot. Richie had a lovely time paddling in the sea, but my heart was in my mouth the whole time lest he get in over his head. Young mothers don't seem to watch their children as we did. All in all, I'm rather glad it's Monday. What about you? Did you enjoy Cats?''

Cats? Surely not—oh, Cats! I let my breath out quietly. "Oh, my, yes, I had no idea it was so good! I knew the music, of course, but the dancing! And the costumes! There was one cat, a Siamese—well, a woman dressed as a cat, of course, but so lean and sinuous and catlike I almost forgot she was human. Was she in the show when you saw it?''

"I don't remember; it's been years. The show's been running forever.''

Indeed. It had been ten years, at least, since I'd seen it myself. I hoped it hadn't changed much, and that I'd remembered enough to sound convincing to people whose memory might be fresher, if anyone should ask.

"Oh, by the way, Louise, the sales staff will all be in this morning at nine on the dot. Mr. Spragge wants to go over some figures with them himself, so they're not to be interrupted until their meeting is over.''

"Got it," I said. That was a piece of luck. I'd thought I might not get a chance to talk to them for sometime, and though it was important that I learn about their Friday night whereabouts, I was beginning not to want to stick around Multilinks a day longer than I had to.

Mr. Pierce and Mrs. Shore came in together, and in a foul mood, both of them. My guess, from the glares they exchanged, was that they'd spent the weekend together and had a lovers' quarrel. Or some kind of quarrel, at any rate.

"*Good* morning," I said with offensive cheeriness. "I hope you both had a pleasant weekend, what with the wonderful weather and all."

Mrs. Shore rolled her eyes, said, "God!" under her breath, and passed me without another word. Mr. Pierce, whose charm appeared to be automatically extended to every female under the age of ninety, stopped and smiled at me.

"Feeling a bit fragile this morning, both of us," he said in a low voice. "You'll have to excuse Vicki. I'm afraid we drank rather a lot too much over the weekend, and we had a filthy row this morning."

Some devil made me say sweetly, "Oh, I didn't know the two of you were married. I mean, different last names and all—"

His smile vanished, and so did the charm. "We're not," he said curtly.

"Oh, I do beg your pardon. Have I put my foot in it?"

"Look, you nosy old cow," he said in a still-lower

tone, but viciously. "If Vicki Shore and I choose to spend a weekend together, it's none of your bleeding business, right? If you want to know all the salacious details, we went to a hotel straight from work on Friday together and have been there ever since, and you can do as you like with that information, including passing it on to Mr. Sanctimonious Spragge! Got it?"

"I'm sure what you do in your own time is your own business, Mr. Pierce," I replied almost as angrily, "so long as you don't do it in the street and frighten the horses. It certainly doesn't seem to have been a very pleasant experience, I must say!"

We glared at each other for a moment, then he shrugged. "Right. Sorry. Not coping too well this morning, am I? Ah, well, it's a great life if you don't weaken."

He went into Evelyn's domain, and I was left wondering why he thought it necessary to go into all those details of what was, as he had pointed out, absolutely none of my business. Was there a slight smell of alibi in the air?

Mr. Dalal and Mr. Upton were the next to arrive, walking in a few seconds apart. Mr. Upton glowered at me but responded briefly to my greeting. Mr. Dalal ignored me and accosted Mr. Upton.

"Please, I must speak to you before we meet with Mr. Spragge. I am very troubled in my mind. You must understand that it is not my fault, this poor sales record. The price of the product must be lowered. Mr. Spragge must be persuaded to do so. The poor countries, they cannot afford to buy at such a high cost.

They tell me this, they say they will buy a competitive product, they say—''

''I do not give a flaming fart what they say!'' said Upton. ''Spragge's not going to do anything about the price, so that's that. It's your bloody job to sell the bloody product, and so far as I can see you couldn't sell blankets to bloody Eskimos. I intend to tell Spragge just that!''

''But there is something peculiar, I tell you, I—''

''If you will come in, gentlemen, Mr. Spragge is waiting.'' Evelyn had appeared in the doorway. She put just the slightest emphasis on ''gentlemen.'' The two quieted and passed into the office.

Evidently I was going to have to wait to find out how they spent their Friday night. If I ever did.

Mr. Hammond presented no problem at all. He came in a few minutes late, twirling his umbrella and doing a little dance step in the hallway.

''Well, you look as though you had a good time this weekend,'' I said brightly.

''Ah, *mais oui!*'' he said in a dreadful French accent. ''Gay Paree and all that, you know?''

''You spent the weekend in Paris?'' I haven't lived long enough in England to find the Paris weekend a commonplace.

''Ooh, la-la! Caught the night shuttle, got there before midnight. And then—'' He rolled his eyes. ''''Thank 'eavens...''' He hummed a few bars of the Maurice Chevalier tune, excruciatingly off-key.

''And now you're all rested and ready for a week of work.'' I grinned at him; he rolled his eyes again and went into the office. Blast it all, he was undoubtedly a reprobate and headed for a fall, but I couldn't help liking Terry Hammond.

Mr. Grey was half an hour late for work, an occurrence that struck me as highly uncharacteristic. He rushed in the door, panting. I suspected he'd run all the way from the Russell Square tube station.

"Goodness, Mr. Grey, you don't look at all well. Did you not have a pleasant weekend?"

"I—no." And with that he vanished through the office door, and I was left with my next question on my lips.

I didn't feel I'd learned very much of interest, and of the two people I most wanted to question, Mr. Fortier probably wouldn't be in at all, and I wasn't sure I had the nerve to tackle the exalted and now highly suspect Mr. Spragge.

Evelyn, however, was another matter. Lunching together seemed to have become an established habit. That Monday being another perfect June day, we bought sandwiches and soft drinks from a little shop and ate our lunch in Russell Square. The pigeons were something of a problem. I despise pigeons and tried to shoo them away, but Evelyn scattered the crumbs of her sandwich, so of course they gathered in droves.

"Oh, I rather like them," she said at my mild protest. "I like all sorts of birds. Just look at how beautiful they are. That lovely soft brown one, for instance, and the gray there, with the black bars on its wings! I've often thought of keeping pigeons, and perhaps racing them, but it takes time to look after them properly, of course. I had a cousin who kept them when we were girls in the country, so I know.''

''What an unusual hobby,'' I commented. ''I think people's hobbies can give one very interesting insights sometimes. You and I love to read mysteries, for example, and we both do some needlework, I believe. Very quiet, sedentary pursuits. But I wonder what a man like Mr. Spragge does in his spare time? Besides gardening, that is.''

Not very subtle, but where Mr. Spragge was concerned, Evelyn was usually willing to talk for hours.

Not this time. ''I'm sure I don't know,'' she said stiffly. ''I have always been given to understand that he has very little spare time. He takes a great deal of work home with him.''

''Really? I haven't seen him taking more than a small attaché case when he leaves.''

Evelyn smiled acidly. ''He does nearly all his work on a computer, of course, either his laptop or the home computer that is linked to the company network. Surely you realize that.''

''Yes, how silly of me. I'm not yet attuned to computers as a principal tool for business, I admit. But surely the poor man must have *some* time free! He can't work every minute.''

''I've always believed he spends a great deal of time with his family and his gardens, and of course his charities.''

''Oh. Oxfam and that sort of thing?''

''No, no.'' She loosened up a little. ''Perhaps I oughtn't to have said charities, for they're not that, exactly. It's simply that he's always taken a keen interest in the problems of the less fortunate, particularly the old colonial countries in India and Africa. Whilst he was up at Oxford, he made a number of friends among the foreign students and became interested in their problems at home, and when he became such a successful businessman, he felt he ought to provide what help he could for others struggling to succeed. So he volunteers his time, oh, hours and hours, in an advisory capacity to small foreign businesses trying to establish themselves, or to grow. Or so he tells me.'' The stiffness returned to her manner. I didn't understand it.

"But surely not on weekends?" I persisted.

"As I told you, I have no idea how he spends his weekends. It's certainly none of my concern."

She shut her mouth firmly, brushed the last of the crumbs from her lap for the ecstatic pigeons, and stood. I'd been put properly in my place, but it didn't worry me much. I might not have learned how Mr. Spragge had spent Friday night, but perhaps I had something more valuable—an excellent reason why Mr. Spragge might be stealing from his own company. Was his idealistic commitment to the struggling poor sufficient motivation for piracy? And was that piracy, or the need for keeping it secret, sufficient motive for murder?

SIXTEEN

I WAS NOW more interested than ever in where Mr. Spragge had been on Friday after work. I felt several things were beginning to come into focus, but I needed some solid evidence. I was trying, between phone calls, to think of an excuse to go into his office when a small crisis arose. Evelyn developed a terrible headache.

I found her at her desk holding a cool cloth to her head. When aspirin and various other remedies did nothing to relieve the pain, I finally persuaded her that she was unfit for work and ought to go home.

"It'll be your hectic weekend taking revenge, I expect," I said as she left. "Now, don't you try to clean up your flat or anything. Go straight to bed."

She promised she would, told me to remind the last men out about locking their doors, and went, looking distinctly ill.

I was sorry she felt so awful, but it gave me the opportunity I needed. I was about to go in to see Mr. Spragge when he came out to see me.

"I'm quite helpless without Evelyn, I'm afraid," he said with a rueful smile. "There was a great deal of dictation to be done, and various other matters for which a skilled secretary is essential."

"Oh, dear," I said, taken aback. "Well, I don't take shorthand, but I would be very happy to try—"

"I'm sure you would, Mrs. Wren, and I appreciate your concern. But Mrs. Forbes knows exactly the way I like things done. No, I've stacks of work to be done at home, and that is where I shall be, if anyone needs me. You do have my home telephone number?"

"Yes, sir," I said. "But isn't it hard to concentrate at home?" I added in one last desperate attempt to learn something—anything. "I mean, your family, your garden—"

He frowned. "A man in my position cannot allow himself to be distracted. My wife fully understands that, and assures me of the peace and quiet I need. Good afternoon, Mrs. Wren."

So. A domestic tyrant as well, perhaps? Interesting, but irrelevant. And I still had no idea where he'd been on Friday.

I was now nearly alone in the office. The entire sales staff, including Mr. Upton, had gone out immediately after their meeting in the morning, presumably with new resolve to pursue customers. I could feel some sympathy for them. Their efforts were essentially doomed.

Mr. Grey and Mr. Hammond, though still working, were sequestered in their own domains. This seemed a good time to try to question Mr. Grey. I thought for a moment and then knocked on his door.

"Yes?"

"I was about to make some tea, Mr. Grey," I said,

poking my head into his office. "I thought a cup might make you feel a little better."

"Thank you, no. I have had severe dyspepsia since Friday night. Tea would only make matters worse."

He did look a little green. Could I write him off, if he'd had some sort of stomach flu all weekend?

Stress can upset the stomach. For a nervous little man like Mr. Grey, snooping around a deserted office would be very stressful.

I sighed. "I'm so sorry. I do hope you recover soon."

No, he was still in the running.

With so few people around, there was (thank heavens!) no one to overhear when I got the phone call. It came in just before six, on Mr. Spragge's private line. I sprinted to Evelyn's desk and picked up the receiver.

"Good afternoon, Multilinks."

"Thank God, an American voice! Who're you?" The voice at the other end was American, too, and extremely irritated.

"I'm only the receptionist. I'm afraid Mr. Spragge is out, and his secretary as well, but I'd be happy to take a message—"

"Not on your damn life! I've been leaving messages for days, and nobody ever calls back. Now listen, lady, whoever you are, I don't care what you have to do to make it happen, but I want to talk to Bill Monahan, and I want to talk to him now!"

For just a few seconds I was struck dumb.

"Hey! Are you there! I said—"

"Yes, I heard you. I'm not—quite sure where to locate Mr. Monahan at the moment."

I wasn't, either. I presumed his body was still in the Thames, or wherever it had been dumped by his murderers. As to the location of his soul, if souls have locations, that was between Mr. Monahan and his maker.

The phone was making angry, frustrated noises. "Yeah, that's the line they've been giving me for two weeks! Now, you get this straight. I know you're just a flunky, but my name is Walt Shepherd. Got that?"

"Yes...and your telephone number?"

"I'm at the home office. In Palo Alto. You've got the number there, but I'll give it to you anyway." The American sequence of numbers gave me a sharp, unexpected stab of homesickness. "And you can tell that boss of yours that unless I hear from Bill by the time I go to bed tonight—that'd be eight in the morning or so, your time—I'm climbing on a plane first thing tomorrow to see what the hell is going on over there!"

"Mr. Shepherd, I—" There was a sharp click before I finished saying the name.

Walt Shepherd. Walt Shepherd. Why did that name sound familiar?

Then the penny dropped, with a very loud clunk. Good grief, Bill Monahan's partner! Now the sole owner of Multilinks, though he didn't know it yet. Dear heaven, now what?

Now was the time to call in the police, that was what. Matters were getting out of control. And I had some proof, now, of the accusations I was about to make. And with a very angry, very high-handed corporate executive getting into the act, I had no real choice left.

Scotland Yard would be the place to call, I supposed. I'd be routed through all kinds of bureaucratic levels until I got to the person I wanted. And the first thing they'd ask me, at all of those levels, was my name. And the second would be why I hadn't told them all of this before.

Well, it would all be very unpleasant, but I'd just have to deal with it. It wasn't entirely my own fault, after all. I'd tried to tell them before.

Yes, and just what was I going to tell them? That there had been a dead man in a train a couple of weeks ago. Why hadn't I reported it? Oh, someone else was to have reported it, yes. And who was this alleged victim? WHO? And what made me think that? Well—because he'd told me about a computer program. No, I couldn't remember the name of it, but my friend had guessed—no, I'd really rather not get my friend involved. Anyway, I knew I was right because the man in question was missing. And what made me think *that?* Because I'd gotten a phone call from his partner. He'd called the Multilinks office here.

Ah. And what were you doing answering the phone at Multilinks? Oh, you were working there, I see. Without a work permit. Without any official documentation whatsoever. Under an assumed name. Yes. And your real name, madam? That's Mrs.—oh, yes, your name is different from your husband's name. And your husband's name?

What in heaven's name would Alan say when he got a call from Scotland Yard asking if he could identify a very suspicious woman masquerading as his wife?

I gritted my teeth and picked up the phone. It would simply have to be done, that's all.

"Oh, Mrs. Wren."

I started guiltily and put the phone down again. Mr. Grey stood by my desk looking disapproving.

"I hope you weren't about to make a personal call, Mrs. Wren. That is not allowed here, you know, not approved at all. Oh, dear, I don't know what might not happen to someone who did that, particularly a new employee. I shouldn't advise it, I really shouldn't."

"I—I was answering a call," I said to his unblinking gaze. "They—it must have been a wrong number."

I sounded as convincing as my fourth-graders whose dogs used to eat their homework.

"Yes, of course."

That was exactly what I used to reply. And I would just look at the child until he turned red and confessed.

I looked at my watch. I was not nine years old, and I wasn't about to be treated as if I were. "It's really past time for me to go home. Was there something you wanted before I leave, Mr. Grey?"

"Oh, you're leaving. I see. Yes, I wanted you to

find some back memos for me, but it can wait until morning. Good night, Mrs. Wren.''

"Good night, Mr. Grey. Don't forget to lock your office door, and close your window. Mrs. Forbes said to remind you.''

"Yes, yes. Mrs. Forbes fusses too much.''

I had to leave after that. I wouldn't have put it past Mr. Grey to be lurking by the door to make sure I didn't place that illicit phone call after all.

Or, perhaps, to listen in.

Well, I wasn't sorry to delay the evil moment a little longer, until I got back to Tom and Lynn's. It might not seem quite so impossible, with them on hand for moral support.

There was, I had discovered that morning, a short-cut to the Underground. If I cut through a narrow passage to one side of the building, I would go past the back gardens of the Multilinks house and the vacant house behind it, on Woburn Place, and avoid the heavy foot traffic on Northampton Way at that time of day. No one ever used the passage, apparently, and I wanted the solitude to think.

There seemed to be an unusual number of crows around, or rooks, or ravens—large black birds, anyway, circling the garden of the vacant house behind Multilinks and cawing hoarsely. I shuddered. They reminded me of a terrifying movie that had given me nightmares for weeks. What, I wondered, had upset the birds?

Or, no, they weren't upset. They were feeding on something. Not a dead cat, I hoped. Nigel had taken the white cat back to Sherebury in an attempt to nurse it back to health, but there were bound to be other strays in the neighborhood. Not really wanting to, I took a closer look in spite of myself.

The body wasn't really very well hidden. The crows had found it easily enough under the bush. All I could see clearly were the feet.

Feet clad in narrow, light brown shoes that looked as though they would pinch.

I suddenly felt very cold, despite the sticky heat of the day. There was a low brick wall on either side of the passage. I groped my way under an overhanging spirea to the wall farthest away from the birds and their meal and sat down, hard. The world was having an alarming tendency to swoop and spin. Better put my head down.

I was in that position when someone came along the path, whistling at first and then suddenly stopping dead still. Something kept me from moving, some instinct like that of a hunted rabbit. I scarcely breathed.

"What the bloody hell—here, get away, you! Shoo!"

My heart did stop beating for an instant, I swear, until I realized he was shouting at the birds. Then there were some rustling noises and a thump. He was over the wall.

"God!" It sounded almost like a prayer, and was followed immediately by a series of retching sounds. I swallowed hard and concentrated on not listening.

Rustles and a thump again, and the sound of feet

running toward Woburn Place. Just when the sounds had almost died away, I heard the cry of "Police! Help! Murder!"

Very quietly, I crept out from under my spirea and walked back to Northampton Way. Whatever my future contact with the police might be, I had no wish to confront them right now over the body of poor Mr. Dalal.

It took all the self-discipline I possessed not to get sick on the Underground. With the heat and the press of humanity—many of whom had not bathed recently, and some of whom were munching on a predinner snack—I have never liked my fellow creatures less than on that ride. One of them came aboard eating something crunchy and greasy that smelled of curry, and I nearly lost it right then.

Fortunately I had only two stops to go, and I managed to make it to the surface, where I stopped, clung to a pillar outside Victoria Station, and inhaled great gasps of the fresher, cooler air. I was very unpopular, obstructing the flow of that great river of men and women hurrying to get home. I didn't greatly care.

I was only ten minutes from the Andersons' house, but I didn't walk there until I'd ducked into the station and bought a bottle of sparkling water. It wasn't cold, but it was wet and clean, and it rinsed the flavor of a good many things out of my mouth. I was able to walk in the front door on Chester Street with a more nearly normal countenance, and in nearly complete control of my digestion.

At least I thought I looked normal, but when Lynn

saw me, she cried out. "Dorothy! What is it? You look like you've seen a ghost!"

"I have," I said. "Or a dead man, anyway. I guess they're not quite the same thing, are they?" I started to laugh and was, in an instant, in the grip of full-fledged hysterics.

Lynn looks rather a lot like Katharine Hepburn, and has a good deal of the same hardheaded, practical approach to life. She wasted no time dithering but ran out of the room and returned in a moment with something that she clapped to the back of my neck and something that she held under my nose. I choked, coughed, and proceeded to get sick in the dishpan that she had also thoughtfully provided, while she sponged my face and held my head.

When, weak and spent and thoroughly ashamed of myself, I had stretched out on her couch, she returned from the bathroom and stood at my side, hands on her hips.

"That's better," she said critically. "You look like hell, but at least you don't look like you're going to pass out."

"Your treatment was very effective," I croaked, my throat raw from vomiting. "What on earth was it?"

"Ice on the back of your neck and ammonia in front of your nose. Together they're an almost sure cure, but sometimes the ammonia makes a person sick."

"Yes, well."

The door of the house, one floor below, opened and closed. "Anybody home?" called Tom.

"Up here." Lynn turned with lean-limbed grace and went to meet him, probably to warn him about their bothersome guest.

Tom can be tactful when he wishes, but he also knows when to go straight to the point. He came upstairs at once, walked into the living room, and looked me straight in the eye.

"A dead man?" he said.

"Could I have something to drink?"

Lynn brought me ginger ale. "No alcohol yet," she decreed. "You've had a shock, and your stomach is still iffy. Ginger ale settles the stomach."

It did seem to, actually. I sipped a little and then, as baldly as possible, told them.

"It wasn't so much the body. I didn't really see anything but his feet, poor little man. It was the crows…"

My voice faded, and Lynn frowned. "Don't talk about them. And don't think anymore about what you saw. That's over and done with. The question is, what do you do now?"

"I think," I said with reluctance, "I think I have to see it through."

There was immediate protest, as I knew there would be, but I felt strong enough now to argue. "All right. You have common sense on your side. I'll admit that. I was almost ready to go to the police this afternoon with all that I knew, or guessed. But don't you see that this murder has changed everything? For one thing, I am now a material witness who has run away. The police wouldn't have been very happy with me before. Now they'd be livid."

"But you're Alan's wife," objected Lynn.

"That doesn't give me the right to break laws, which I have assuredly done. And I don't want to involve Alan if I can possibly help it. He may be retired, officially, but he's still very active in police work, and think what the scandal sheets would do with this! Besides, I'm still incognito at that office. How long do you think that would last if the police knew my name?"

"They'll know soon enough, anyway," put in Tom. "They'll be swarming all over Multilinks tomorrow morning, talking to everyone."

"Not until they identify Mr. Dalal, they won't, and that may not be for some time. I can't imagine that the murderers would have left any identification on the body."

"Am I to take it you have no intention of helping them with the identification process?" Tom's voice was very dry.

"I do not." Mine was fully as arid. "Lynn, I'm really feeling much better. Do you think I could have a little something in this revolting stuff—or instead of it?"

Lynn complied, I suspect with the intent of lowering my resistance, for after I'd had a sip or two of bourbon, she returned to the attack.

"Dorothy, you simply *can't* go back to that place!

Do have a little sense. They're killing people left and right!''

"But they have no reason to kill me," I said patiently. "They don't know who I am, they have absolutely no reason to connect me with that woman on the train who saw Bill Monahan, and even if they did, they don't know that woman poses any threat to them.''

"They know someone was snooping the other night," said Lynn.

"Maybe. Maybe not. But they don't know it was me, or I'd be out on my ear. Listen, Lynn, this thing is about to come to a head, I'm sure of it, and with any luck at all I'm going to have everything buttoned up in a day or two. I can look after myself for that long.''

The argument went on for another drink or two, wandering from the point as our minds lost a little of their focus. Tom was finally moved to exact a promise from me.

"All right. I can see you're determined to have your own way, D. And I admit you've been right often enough in the past to have a point. But I am absolutely going to the police with this on—what's today, Tuesday?''

"Monday," said Lynn, as I wailed, "But, Tom!''

"—am going to the police on Thursday morning with the whole story unless you've managed to work out the mess by then, D. And I'll go tomorrow unless you'll promise me, faithfully, to back out at the first sign of personal danger. Agreed?''

Reluctantly, I agreed.

SEVENTEEN

I NEVER PROMISED, though, to let Tom and Lynn in on everything I was doing. I had some ideas up my sleeve that I was pretty sure they wouldn't like, but it was time to take some direct action. I was tired of simply gathering information.

I sneaked down to the kitchen after the two of them had been in bed for a while. I didn't dare make real coffee; they might smell it. But I rummaged in the cupboards, discovered an elderly jar of instant espresso tucked away in a corner, and made myself a very strong cup of it. It tasted terrible, but the jolt of caffeine helped chase away the effects of a difficult day and a fair amount of bourbon.

I waited an hour. Surely they'd be sound asleep by now. Moving as quietly as I could, I went into Tom's study and looked up a number in the phone book.

I am a rabid Anglophile. I admit it. I love its castles and villages, its people, its roses. I wallow in its history and culture, and I love the bustle and excitement of London.

There are aspects of England, however, that I do not admire, and one of them is its gutter press. English presses publish some of the finest newspapers in the world, but they also publish some of the very worst. And winning the award for sleaze and sensationalism, hands down, is the *Daily World.*

"Good evening, *Daily World,* may I help you?" The bored young man sounded as if he hoped he couldn't.

"I want to speak to a news editor."

"Yes, madam. And your name?"

"Never mind about my name," I said, trying to Anglicize my accent as much as possible. "Do you want my news or not?"

A sigh. "That would depend on what it is, madam. If you've just spotted Elvis or Diana or aliens, or all of the above together, then not tonight, thank you."

"No. This is real news, not idiotic nonsense, and it's important. Just you tell someone who can do something about it that Bill Monahan is missing."

"Bill—you don't mean *the* Bill Monahan?"

"I mean the American computer magnate, that's who I mean. You ring up the London office of Multilinks tomorrow, and if they can tell you where he is, I'll eat every copy of the *Daily World* for the next week."

I hung up on the rapid-fire questions of the no longer bored reporter. The *World* has a reputation for printing anything, if it's juicy enough, without bothering about verification. I hoped they lived up to their reputation.

The *World* is a morning paper. Millions of British men and women consume its meal of the salacious and the sensational with their breakfast. By the time the Multilinks offices opened on Tuesday morning, the fur should be flying. Unless I was very badly misinformed about journalistic practices, reporters would be lying in wait for the office staff. I hoped, very much I hoped, that I'd disguised my accent well enough so they wouldn't spot me as their anonymous tipster.

I had one other phone call to make, but that one had to wait until morning, and given the timing, there was no way I could conceal it from Tom and Lynn. I stumbled down to breakfast, groggy from too little sleep, and placed the call even before I'd finished my coffee.

"Hello, Nigel? Sorry to call so early."

"'S'all right. I wasn't asleep." A yawn came clearly over the line.

"I'll bet you were. I need some information, as soon as you can get it. You have a computer at home, don't you?"

"Yes." He was alert now.

"Well then, can you look up airline schedules for me?"

"Going on holiday, are you?"

"No, and it's too early in the day for sarcasm, young man. I want you to find out how early a plane leaving San Francisco today might get here."

"San Francisco to London, today. Any particular airline?"

"No, just the earliest flight. It's about midnight there now, so I should think nothing would leave for several hours, but I need to know. As soon as you can, Nigel."

"Right. I'll ring you back."

It took about ten minutes. I marveled again at the amazing resources a computer could command.

"I checked all the major airlines that fly into Heathrow or Gatwick from San Francisco. The earliest flight out is at six-forty their time, arriving six-forty tomorrow at Gatwick. No one with any sense would take that one, though, because it has a very long connection in Atlanta. There are three or four much later ones that arrive between seven and eight. Nothing any earlier."

"*Thank* you, Nigel!" I did some rapid mental arithmetic. Given the time it takes to clear immigration and collect baggage, and then the journey from the airport into London, I had something over twenty-four hours before Mr. Shepherd arrived in London breathing fire. Unless…

"Nigel, one more thing. Do you think it's likely that Multilinks has a corporate jet?"

"They didn't a month ago, at any rate. I've been reading all I could get my hands on about them, and one of the magazines specifically mentioned that they were nearing that stage, but hadn't quite got there."

"Good! Very good! We're coming around the homestretch, Nigel! I have to go to work now, but I'll call you later if I get a chance and bring you up to speed. Oh! No, wait—I've just had a thought."

"If that tone of voice means what I think it means, I'm not quite sure I want to hear your idea." His own voice held the liveliest apprehension.

"Nothing dire, I promise. Just—you do still have that cat, don't you? Sneaky Pete?"

"Yes, I brought him home with me. Well, I couldn't simply turn him out when he was starving, could I? And Inga's taken a fancy to the old reprobate. He's not actually bad looking, now that he's cleaned himself up a bit. He can see out of both eyes now, and he's beginning to fatten up."

I grinned a little. Why do men so often sound defensive when they're caught falling in love with an animal? "Do you suppose you could take some time off today and come to London? With the cat?"

Nigel groaned. "He howled all the way home last Saturday."

"Call my vet—Mr. Douglas, he's in the book—and have him give Pete a tranquilizer. Can you come?"

A sigh. "I might get away this afternoon, if you really think—"

"I do. Come straight to the Multilinks office. I'll spring for cab fare if you don't want to take the cat on the tube. Come as soon as you can, and definitely before the office closes at six."

"You're going to lay a trap, aren't you?"

"I'm certainly going to try." I hung up.

"What was that about?" asked Lynn, who had listened openly and avidly.

"I had a call yesterday. I forgot to tell you about it in all the other excitement." I told them about Walt Shepherd and his threat to jump on the first plane. "And we've missed his deadline, so I suppose he really will do just that. He sounded as if he meant it."

"Whew!" Tom whistled. "And when he gets here the—er—spit *will* hit the fan!"

"With a vengeance. The police will get dragged in, then, and I'll have to confess what I've been up to. That's why I wanted to know when he's apt to arrive. Not till tomorrow morning at the earliest, according to Nigel, so I thought I'd better speed up the action at the office. Time to flush them out, I think."

"*What* are you going to do, Dorothy?" Lynn's voice was full of awful foreboding.

"I've already done part of it, in fact. Read your newspapers, dear hearts. See you later!"

I waved blithely and sailed out the door.

I must have called the *World* very close to their deadline the night before, for the front page looked like a hasty remake. "TYCOON MISSING!!!" screamed a banner head three inches tall. I bought a copy and read it with great enjoyment on the tube. There was no hint that the story was the purest rumor. It sounded authoritative as could be. "Our sources" sounded much better than "an anonymous phone call."

After I'd read the account twice, I scanned the paper carefully for the other story, the dead man in the garden. As I had suspected, the body remained unidentified. The man who had reported the murder worked in a nearby office but could make no identification, and there was nothing useful in the dead man's clothing. Good. The police would undoubtedly come around today, because our back garden was adjacent to the one where the body was found, but I doubted they had yet connected the dead man specifically with Multilinks. He looked more like an impoverished student, and I guessed they'd be checking the University of London first.

I carefully left the paper on the train for others to enjoy and pass along.

A solid phalanx of reporters surrounded the entrance to Multilinks. I could see and hear them the moment I rounded the corner into Northampton Way. (I had decided it was better not to take the shortcut anymore. I didn't want to put ideas in anybody's head.) They descended on me as I tried to climb the steps, and even after I claimed to be an unimportant temporary employee who'd never heard of Mr. Monahan (a statement that was at least half true), still they pushed and shoved and shouted. I suffered something akin to a panic attack when I discovered the door was locked. I rang the bell frantically and fell through it the minute Mrs. Forbes opened it for me.

Evelyn was in a state, literally wringing her hands as we walked together into her office. "Whew!" I said, flinging myself on the couch. "I feel like I've been in a football scrimmage. What in the world is *that* all about!"

"Oh, Mrs. Wren! You didn't tell them anything, did you?"

"I didn't know anything to tell. Who's Bill Monahan?"

I thought she was going to faint. "He's the founder

of Multilinks! Oh, this is terrible! Mr. Spragge will be so upset!''

''But, Ev—Mrs. Forbes, what's *happened?*''

''Nothing! Nothing at all! It's a nasty rumor, that's all!''

Eventually I got her calmed down enough for coherence. According to her, Monahan was bound to be at home in America where he belonged, but they couldn't phone him at this hour. It would be a little after one in the morning in San Francisco, where he apparently lived in a luxuriously renovated Victorian house, and no one at this end had the courage to wake up the big boss. (She didn't put it quite that way, but she was obviously frightened.) At the very first moment the poor man might be expected to be out of bed in San Francisco, she personally would ring him at his home and scotch the rumors. That, however, could not be done until afternoon, London time.

''And oh, I don't know what this will do to business, or to the stock offering! I hardly know how to face Mr. Spragge!''

I had the feeling business wasn't going to be Mr. Spragge's primary worry. The noose, it seemed to me, was tightening rapidly around his neck. If he hadn't informed even his confidential secretary that Monahan was expected in the London office, he must have been planning from the very first to kill him.

I didn't, of course, express any of these thoughts to Mrs. Forbes. For one thing, I could be wrong, and for another, I was genuinely unhappy about the whole situation. Mr. Spragge, despite the contradictions in his character, struck me as a likable man, an idealist gone wrong. Well, idealists throughout history have often been very dangerous people.

I had still had no proof, of course, of anything except that Bill Monahan was in fact missing. I hoped, by watching and listening very carefully—and with the help of Sneaky Pete—to be able to prove a lot more before the day was out.

For the first hour or two that Tuesday morning, no business at all got done. The big dailies all checked in, though over the phone, thank goodness, not on the premises. One after another: *Times, Telegraph, Guardian, Standard,* others I didn't recognize. Evelyn told them all the same thing: rumor, no truth in it, would telephone Monahan as soon as it was morning in California. The tabloids, outside, got very little satisfaction out of anybody, but they did shoot one or two pictures that considerably unnerved their victims, poor little Mr. Grey and a shaken Mr. Spragge.

All in all, though the hubbub was annoying, I thought my ploy was working quite well. Someone in this office had a great deal to hide, and concealment is much harder when the nerves are shattered.

The police arrived about ten-thirty, in the person of two very polite individuals from Scotland Yard who talked to all of us about the body in the garden. My interview, though brief, was a test of my own nerves; this time I was the one who had something to conceal, and I had never before (barring perhaps an incident or two in America, concerning parking meters) lied to the police.

However, I was prepared for the kind of questions they would ask, and my answers were absolutely truthful except on two crucial points: the route I took leaving the office, and whether I had seen or heard anything unusual. (Well, of course I didn't tell them my real name, but surely that was minor?) They were apparently satisfied; at any rate, they went on from me to the more important members of the firm after only a few minutes. I was very careful not to relax for several seconds after they left the room, and then only gradually; I remembered an Agatha Christie book in which relaxing too soon was a liar's undoing!

I'd have given a great deal to eavesdrop while the others were questioned, but the geography and solid construction of the office made that impossible. The best I could hope for was a recap later from everybody. I'd bring the subject up, anyway, which should be easy enough. Given the climate of the office that day, not to talk about the various crises would have been abnormal.

After the police left and the reporters gave up, the office seemed very silent, the silence of a heavy, still day just before a storm. The weather was in fact still beautiful—outside, that is. Inside, the barometer seemed to be falling fast.

Perhaps it was only my overstrained imagination. There was no particular reason for uproar, now that all our tormentors had left. The noisiest of the staff, those in sales, were all out, including Mr. Upton. Mr. Dalal, of course, would never be in again, but I tried to wash that thought out of my brain; it was something only the murderer ought, at this stage, to know. The murderer, I mused. Mr. Fortier hadn't come in. Did that mean anything, or was he simply following his usual pattern? If he read the papers, one would think he'd have shown up, if only for an urgent conference with Spragge. I shook my head in irritation. That kind of speculation was utterly fruitless. My time would be much better spent seeking some real information.

Mr. Grey seemed, when I passed his door, to be working hard, sitting hunched over his computer in an appalling posture. No wonder he was so round-shouldered. Mr. Hammond, too, was working, though not as usual. He usually whistled, cheerfully and off-key. Today he was subdued.

I stopped at his desk. "Did the police give you a hard time?"

He entered a figure, clicked the mouse, and turned away from the computer. "Not particularly. What about you?"

"Not too bad. I was so nervous, I'm sure they thought I was lying, though."

"Not had many dealings with the police, eh?"

I laughed merrily with him. If he only knew!

"Now me," he went on, "I've been in the slammer a few times. I like me beer, see? And me wine."

"And your women, and your song," I added irresistibly.

"Well—yeah. You know how it is! But this time I 'ain't done nuffink,' as they say, so I told the truth like a good little boy."

"What did they ask you?"

"Same as you, I expect. Did I see or hear anything unusual, which way did I go when I left here, and that."

"Which way *did* you go?"

"Northampton Way to Russell Square, to the tube. I left just after you, I thought, but I didn't see you. Which way did *you* go?"

"The other way," I lied fluently. "To Euston. I was meeting a friend. I didn't see or hear anything, either. Did you?"

The telephone ringing madly at my desk cut his reply to a shake of the head as I dashed away.

I wasn't sure how to tackle the inscrutable Mr. Grey, but to my surprise he raised the questions himself. He came out to my desk to ask me for an old file, and lingered.

"Where did you go when you left here last night, Mrs. Wren?"

I repeated the story I'd told Mr. Hammond. "Why?" I added.

"It's only that you must have left just before the alarm was turned in. About that unfortunate man, you know. I wondered if you'd noticed anything unusual."

"The police asked me that, of course. I said no. Did you?"

"Oh, no," he said hastily. "My room is at the front of the house. What would I have seen?"

"Search me," I said. "Somebody walking past your window, or turning into the passageway—" Belatedly, I shut up. He might very well have seen someone. Me!

"As a matter of fact—I did rather think I saw you going in that direction. I can't see the entrance to the passage from where I sit, but surely if you were going to Euston…"

He let the phrase trail off suggestively. I hoped I looked annoyed rather than upset.

"Well, as a matter of fact, I did turn in that direction first. I had forgotten about my friend. I have a terrible memory. But I remembered before I'd gone very far and came back. Surely you saw me return!" I said aggressively. Attack is the best defense.

"No, I—I was away from my desk for a few moments."

Just like Mr. Grey not to admit he had to go to the bathroom like normal human beings! But, I thought when he finally left, if he saw me possibly heading toward the passage and did nothing about it, he must not have had anything on his conscience.

Except why was he being so picky about it?

Because it's in his nature to be picky, I replied wearily to myself. A dislike for the man is insufficient reason to believe he's a murderer.

I was just coming out of the bathroom, before lunch, when the storm that had been brewing all morning broke. Evelyn was in Mr. Spragge's office and had, most unusually for her, left his door ajar.

Her voice was high and nervous and carried easily to where I was, only inches from the door. Praying

no one else would feel the call of nature, I stood
stock-still, scarcely daring to breathe.

"Mr. Spragge. May I ask if you have any reason
to be dissatisfied with my work?"

I couldn't hear his answer, low and rumbling, but
there was, I thought, surprise in the inflections of his
voice.

"Well, then, why are you so annoyed with me?"
She sounded close to tears. Again Spragge's voice
carried surprise and, perhaps, a little impatience.

"I've—I've done my best to support your work.
All your work, as you know, sir. I've been loyal to
you. But if I am to be rewarded with *this*—"

"With *what?*" Now his voice was raised enough
that I could hear.

"With—with mistrust and impatience and—and—
Mr. Spragge, I'm sorry, but I must ask you. Who was
with you in this office on Friday night?"

I didn't wait to hear his answer, but fled like a
scalded cat.

EIGHTEEN

I HAD INTENDED to ask Evelyn to lunch with me, but I had too much to think about now. A solitary break, with time to think, would be better. I got food at a take-out place, took it into one of the little gardens that abound in the area, and sat down to worry.

Of course, I reasoned as I ate something and drank something without particularly noticing what they were, neither Evelyn nor Mr. Spragge had reason to be suspicious of me, even after they had straightened out their cross-purposes and Spragge had convinced Evelyn that he had not been in the office Friday night. True, I had asked to stay late that night, but "late" wouldn't normally translate to nine-thirty or so. And what reason would Louise Wren, brand-new employee, have to stick around for hours on a Friday night and snoop in the office?

No, they didn't really know a thing, except that someone—two someones; Evelyn had plainly heard Nigel's voice as well—who had no business there had been in Spragge's office at a decidedly unusual hour.

For that matter, I suddenly stopped to think, what had Evelyn been doing there? It must have been she, of course, who'd let in the cat. Wait, though—it was coming—of course! She'd told me herself, but I'd been too stupid to listen carefully enough. Her daughter's train had been very late, at Euston Station. Evelyn had had to wait for it. And she'd been worried about the office doors being locked.

It was no more than a fifteen-minute walk from Euston to the office. She could very naturally have walked there to kill some time and check the doors, and when she found someone in the office, she…

There I ran aground. She what? As conscientious as Evelyn Forbes was, why didn't she just march on into Spragge's office and catch us in the act? Or call the police? *Why* would she just leave?

I ran over her questions to Spragge again, and once again, and when I finally got it, pity welled up in me and I put down the food I didn't want anymore.

She thought it was Spragge in there, with a woman.

Spragge, whom she idolized. Spragge, who was married to an invalid. Spragge, who was a churchwarden. Spragge, carrying on with a floozy.

Nigel and I had been nervous, I remembered. We had giggled a little, quietly. And we had spoken in low tones. Yes, with a little curdled imagination the sounds could certainly have been misinterpreted. The office door, I had reason to know, was heavy, the walls solid. Even with the door ajar, I had been able to hear only Evelyn just now, until Spragge raised his voice.

That poor woman! I could have told her the idol almost certainly had feet of clay, but she wouldn't have listened to me. It would have seemed like betrayal. Coming to the same conclusion herself, she had felt betrayed. And now, now that she had shown

Spragge her suspicions and he had denied any knowledge of what she was talking about—my toes curled. Of all the embarrassments in the world, few go quite as deep as the revelation of unrequited love.

For love was, I was quite sure, what Evelyn felt for Spragge. She probably didn't know it. She was probably prepared to swear it was only admiration, sympathy, and loyalty.

Or she could have sworn it until now. Now that she had recognized her own jealousy, she could no longer pretend, even to herself.

Poor woman!

I didn't want to go back to the office at all, but two things kept me from running away. I reminded myself that I was no nearer catching a murderer, and I had only a little more time. The answer was in that office somewhere; that was one reason I went back.

The other was that Evelyn deserved some support. I couldn't say anything to her, of course. I wasn't supposed to know anything about the whole sorry business. But if she wanted someone to talk to, a shoulder to cry on, I was a safe sort of person, as a near-stranger, and a foreigner at that. And another woman.

Against every instinct I possessed, I turned my steps to Northampton Way.

Evelyn wasn't there when I returned. I supposed she had either gone out to lunch or taken the rest of the day off to regain her composure. I hoped it was the latter, but I doubted it. Her strong sense of duty had almost kept her at the office yesterday in spite of a disabling headache. She would probably consider giving way to an emotional upset to be the act of a coward—letting down the side, not keeping a stiff upper lip—all the clichés that make the English so admirable, so reliable, and, sometimes, so foolish.

Mr. Hammond had also left, and Mr. Grey did so as soon as I returned, muttering something about inconsiderate people who lingered over their lunches while others waited. (I was ten minutes early getting back.) I knocked on Mr. Spragge's door to see if he was in. Rather to my surprise, he was. "Oh, I didn't mean to disturb you, but Evelyn seems to have gone to lunch, and I wanted to know if you can take phone calls."

"Calls? Oh yes, yes, by all means." He smiled halfheartedly. "Mrs.—er—"

"Wren."

"Mrs. Wren, have you noticed anything—er—odd about Mrs. Forbes? I realize you hardly know her, but I wondered…" He trailed off helplessly.

"We've begun to be friends," I answered guardedly. "She's a very nice woman, isn't she?"

"Indeed, indeed. But of late she has seemed…" He made a vague gesture.

"I did think she seemed quite upset this morning, but of course with police and reporters all over the place, we were all somewhat upset."

"Yes, yes, perhaps that explains it." He was speaking almost to himself. I waited. "Thank you, Mrs. Wren," he said after a moment, blinking and remembering I was there. I went back to my own desk and thought about the unlikely passions that stir human-kind.

Then I pulled myself together. There is a time for philosophical musings, but this wasn't it. I had far more important things to think about. In between phone calls from the press, which had slowed down to a trickle, and business calls, which were almost nonexistent, I tried to consider what I knew.

Put that way—what I *knew*—it didn't really amount to a lot. I knew that Bill Monahan was dead. I knew that someone at Multilinks was pirating copies of very expensive software. I knew that Evelyn Forbes had returned to the office Friday night, that Vicki Shore was having an affair with Lloyd Pierce, that Brian Upton took drugs and had a temper, that Terry Hammond drank too much.

Did any of that hang together? Did most of it matter?

Those were among the questions I couldn't answer. And time was growing short.

Take another tack. I was reasonably certain that Mr. Spragge was the pirate, stealing from his own company to save the world. Or he'd started out that way. Was it cynical to assume that money, a great deal of it, now entered into his calculations? Not to mention the megalomania that lies in wait for all capable men who start playing God.

I wished Mr. Spragge would go out to lunch so I could have a look in his office. His was the one that mattered most, and Nigel and I had been interrupted before we could go over it carefully. Maybe if I could figure out a way to stick around tonight—but no, Evelyn would be suspicious. I couldn't have her getting ideas about me and spreading them around the office. Someone, I had to keep reminding myself, someone in this place, at least one of these ordinary-looking people, was a murderer. Probably my empathetic, charming churchwarden of a boss.

At least I could check Fortier's office again. We'd given it up as a bad job, Nigel and I; it was too much of a mess, and we'd had little light. If I were quiet, I could surely poke around in his desk for a while now. If Mr. Spragge heard me, I could always claim Fortier had called and asked me to find something for him. I wouldn't have much time, but I might get lucky.

It didn't take me long, after all, and I had little need to be quiet. I stole into the back office, shuddering a little as I passed the file cabinet used by poor Mr. Dalal. If it hid any secrets, they didn't matter now, did they? Mr. Dalal, I was sure, had been killed because he talked too much, killed because he thought something funny was going on at Multilinks. How right he had been!

And I, who *knew* something funny was going on, had better keep my eyes open and stay on my guard. I crept to Fortier's desk, knelt in front of it (my knees protesting loudly), and opened the big bottom drawer on the right.

Nothing. It was empty. I sat back on my heels, frowning. I couldn't remember what had been in that drawer Friday night, but it had been stuffed full of something. All the drawers had been.

I tried another, and yet another, in growing alarm, until I had opened and very quietly shut every drawer in his desk.

They were all empty. Mr. Fortier had cleaned out his desk.

He'd done a bunk.

I sat there, ignoring my tortured knees, frozen in horror. Flight is a sign of guilt. I'd waited too long, tried too hard to prove my suspicions. Had I let a murderer flee, perhaps out of the country to his native Canada?

Getting hastily to my feet, every joint creaking in protest, I went to his file cabinet, opened it, and then had to hold on to keep myself upright when I sagged with relief. The files were still full. That must mean that he hadn't finished the cleanup operation, that he was coming back. True, he might have decided to leave some of the business paperwork, but there were personal things here too, I saw in a quick glance— letters, phone numbers—that I thought he'd want. If I were a criminal fleeing from justice, I'd take along everything that might possibly give any hints about me. I devoutly hoped that Mr. Fortier was smart enough to do the same, because otherwise...

My mind occupied with wild speculations, I was nearly caught. I missed hearing Evelyn's return to the office until her footsteps approached the door of the office I was illicitly occupying. I closed the file drawer hastily and made it almost to the door before she came in.

"Why, Mrs. Martin! Whatever are you doing in here?"

She had been crying, but her cheeks were dry now and her voice steady.

"I had a call from someone, a customer I suppose, who's very anxious to reach Mrs.—I mean Ms. Shore. I was looking to see if she kept a schedule of her appointments in here somewhere, but I couldn't find one."

Evelyn pursed her lips. "I believe Mr. Upton has the only copy, and of course he is not in today, either." Her tone was extremely acid. "You had better let me take the call."

"They said they'd call back," I improvised.

"Hmph! Man or woman?"

"Man."

"Yes, I might have suspected. Customer, indeed!"

She marched on into the room and looked around with distaste. "Really! Look at this place! You'd think these salespeople were pigs, the way they leave everything lying about. I suppose I should try to tidy up."

Ah. A chance to talk. "I'd be glad to help, if—"

The look she gave me wouldn't have flattered a large hairy spider. "I'm sure you have enough to do, Mrs. Wren. Some of these documents are confidential."

Ouch! Evelyn's misery had soured to fury, it seemed, radiating from her, scorching everyone within range. Not a good time for conversation, then, but I kept trying. "I don't actually have a lot to do.

The phone doesn't seem to be ringing much this afternoon. I hate to just sit idle.''

"Oh, for heaven's sake, do anything you like! Read a book, if you really can't find something more productive. You'll find one or two in my bottom file drawer. But please leave me to my work!''

I got out of her way as quickly as possible. I didn't have the least desire to read, but I took her up on her offer and carried a fat Tom Clancy I hadn't read back to my desk and sat with it closed in my lap while I tried to think. Eventually I drew out a stenographer's notebook someone had left behind in a bottom drawer and began to make notes in a semi-shorthand.

Cs. Anti, I headed a page.

Under it I listed the Multilinks staff by initials and began to set down abbreviated versions of the case against them.

Terry Hammond was first. He couldn't be the doctor on the train. His hands shook, his hair was red, his accent was wrong. But he had good reason to be the pirate. His drinking could cost him his job, had probably cost him others.

On the other hand, I liked him, darn it.

That all went down as:

TH. Not MD.—hands and hair. Pir? Booze, $. But—

It finished with a smiley face.

Brian Upton was next. He wasn't the doctor either; his accent was entirely wrong. He had, though, far better reasons to be the pirate. Drugs cost a lot of money, and he was being blackmailed. A good possibility. A couple of plus signs ended his entry.

Mr. Grey. I couldn't even remember his first name. He had the right sort of accent and he looked like anybody else in a dark suit. But he was such a Mr. Milquetoast! Unless that was all a front, and he was a consummate actor, he was out of it. I put down a firm minus sign.

Vicki Shore. Well, she certainly wasn't the doctor, but I liked her as the pirate, partly because I didn't like her at all. (A smiley face with a diagonal bar through it.) She was a thoroughly unpleasant woman whose husband apparently held the purse strings, and she wanted money to make whoopie. Another couple of plus signs.

Lloyd Pierce. He could have been the doctor. Right appearance, right accent, quite enough chutzpah to carry it off. And he had reason for piracy; it costs a good deal to be a womanizer. He and Vicki working together? It couldn't be dismissed.

I looked at my notebook with its cryptic entries and sighed. I was just playing games, really. Oh, everything I'd noted was reasonable enough. But to set against it:

Fortier. Fortier, who had cleaned out his desk. Fortier, who had been terrified by a simple question on the phone about Bill Monahan. Fortier, with a faint Canadian accent. Fortier, who would do anything his boss asked him to.

There wasn't really much doubt, was there, that Fortier was the doctor on the train? Or that he had, either with Spragge or at his orders, murdered Monahan?

And Spragge. The boss. The brains behind the whole business. I couldn't doubt it any longer. It hadn't been any of the sales staff; they didn't have a clue what was making the orders evaporate. It hadn't been nice Terry Hammond or gray little Mr. Grey. It was Spragge himself, with his laptop computer and his need for complete control. Spragge the rose grower, Spragge the churchwarden, Spragge the idol of his secretary.

And how, how, how was I to prove it?

I tore the notebook pages into tiny pieces and dropped them in the wastebasket.

THERE WAS A little flurry of phone calls about two-thirty. Some of the newspapers had followed up with calls to California now that it was morning there, and having been unable to reach Monahan either at home—no answer—or at his office—no cooperation—were calling back to pester us. I took it upon myself to fend them off. Evelyn was upset enough, and I'd accomplished all I could in the way of flurrying Mr. Spragge. It hadn't been enough, but more pressure wouldn't help. I didn't know if Evelyn had tried to place the promised call to Monahan at home, and I didn't ask. She plainly didn't want to talk, at least not to me, and I really pitied her and didn't intend to increase her difficulties.

I had forgotten all about Nigel and the cat until they showed up a little after five, the cat in a carrier this time and quite silent. They created an immediate crisis.

I had intended to use the cat to unmask the person who had been in the office Friday night. I'd thought perhaps the beast would recognize the person it had followed into the building, or the person would recognize the cat and make some sort of damaging admission.

Now the only person likely to be damaged was me, if the cat was friendly to me—and Evelyn saw it and made some connection.

"Nigel, you've got to get it out of here! Right now!" My voice was an anguished whisper. "I'm sorry, but things have changed—*Pete, be quiet!*"

For the cat, perhaps at the sound of my voice, had started to meow loudly.

"Nigel—"

It was too late. The cat's cries resounded loudly through the office. Mr. Grey came out. Mr. Hammond came out. And Evelyn came out, extremely annoyed.

"Mrs. Wren! What is the meaning of this disturbance?"

With a mental apology to Nigel, I looked indignant and said, "I haven't the slightest idea. This young man came in here with this cat, and it started to yowl. I don't know what he's doing here, and I certainly don't know why he brought that cat with him!"

NINETEEN

EVIDENTLY PETE WAS insulted by my reference to "that cat," because he uttered a comment or two that were certainly not complimentary, and then proceeded to escape from his carrier and jump onto my desk, knocking the telephone to the floor and scattering papers everywhere. In the commotion that followed as everyone tried to apprehend the fugitive, Nigel acquitted himself nobly. He might not have been a star in his school's dramatic productions, but he should have been awarded an Oscar on the spot for his performance that afternoon.

He caught Pete, who had ended his flight by diving under my desk and rubbing against my ankles, stuffed him back into the box (incurring a scratch or two in the process), and apologized charmingly. "Sorry, ladies—gentlemen. Didn't mean to cause a row. I live in the next street, you see, and this old chap's rather been coming round lately. I'd as soon take him in as not—I like cats—but I thought I'd best see if he belongs to anyone. As I can see he doesn't belong here, I'll apologize for the disturbance and take myself off."

"He certainly," Evelyn said with a sniff, "seems to have taken to Mrs. Wren."

"I like cats myself," I murmured, while casting

bitter mental imprecations Pete's way. "They can always tell, can't they?"

I had managed when the confusion was at its height to scribble a quick note to Nigel. "Go to Tom and Lynn's. See you there later." Now I saw him and his noisy friend to the door, mouthed a quick "Sorry," and slipped the note into his hand.

I thought six o'clock would never get there, but Evelyn finally came out of her office to inform me, coldly, that she was staying late, but I was free to leave. I jumped at the chance. I had decided that Nigel and I would have to come back for some more reconnaissance, and had set the Yale lock on the back door in the unlocked position, on the off chance that Evelyn wouldn't notice. An unlocked door would make matters easier, but I was prepared to break a window if I had to. Tomorrow was D day; I had to have some solid evidence by then.

I had expected to find Nigel in a fine Welsh rage, but I had reckoned without Lynn. If any social situation has ever caught her unprepared, I've never seen it. When I finally got there, she and Nigel were sitting in the living room over beer and snacks, while the cat, purring loudly, was devouring a dish of what looked remarkably like pâté de foie gras.

"Nigel, I *am* sorry! Plans backfired." I poured myself a drink and joined them, explaining what had been going on all day.

"And I don't blame Evelyn for being upset, or for taking it out on me, but if she'd happened to notice the cat that night, and then had put two and two together today, we'd both have been in the soup, Nigel,'' I concluded.

"We still could be," he said, "if she does her sums between now and tomorrow morning."

"You're all too right," I said, rolling my eyes to the ceiling. "That's why we have to go back to the office tonight and find some definitive proof of Spragge's guilt."

"Like what?"

"I don't know. That's the trouble. We know he's the one who's pirating the software, maybe with Fortier's help. Fortier's in it up to his neck, that's certain, or he wouldn't be about to decamp. But I still don't know which of them was the actual murderer. For all I know, they both are. Maybe one of them took care of Monahan, and the other dispatched poor little Mr. Dalal!"

I was sounding a little frantic by that time, I suppose, and maybe not terribly convincing. But Nigel didn't have to hoot with laughter.

"Right! Two murderers. Spot on, Dorothy. You'll be saying it's the whole company, next—one of those plots where everybody did it!"

"All right, laugh! But unless we can figure out exactly what's been going on, and find it before tomorrow…"

Lynn groaned. "Tomorrow the police are going to move in, and it's all going to blow up in your face, Dorothy!"

"Not if I can come up with something tonight, it isn't. If I can provide Mr. Whatever-His-Name-Is—"

"Shepherd," said Nigel, and I made a face at him.

"—okay, Shepherd. If I can show him some solid proof that his partner is dead and Fortier and Co. killed him, Scotland Yard won't know what hit 'em. But I have to have proof, and I don't propose to get it alone. Are you with me, Nigel?"

"Oh, *no* you don't, Dorothy! Not *this* time."

"Lynn, I have to go—you must see that!"

"Of *course* you do. And Nigel's *panting* to go with you. But Tom and I are coming along, and I *won't* listen to a word of argument. Aren't we, darling?"

Tom, who walked in just at that moment, grinned at her. "You betcha. Are what?"

"Are going with Dorothy and Nigel to find a clue."

Then Tom had to be brought up to speed, which took us most of dinner. To Lynn's surprise, I think, I didn't argue about including the two of them in the expedition. The dimensions of the search were daunting, after all, and Nigel and I could well use extra hands and eyes.

So we didn't prolong our meal (which was a pity, because Lynn's meals deserve loving attention), and we saved the after-dinner drinks for later. We were lucky that the weather had turned murky again, for on a clear June night it wouldn't have been really dark until after ten, and we had too much to do to wait that long.

"It's actually midsummer night, did you know?" said Nigel as we left the house.

"It's to be hoped we won't behave like Bottom and crew and make asses of ourselves," said Lynn.

We drove; it would be so late when we were ready to leave the office that a cab would be hard to find— and parking wasn't a problem in that area at night. Besides, we might find ourselves wanting to get away in a hurry!

Tom parked his elegant BMW a few doors away from the Multilinks office. We saw no need to advertise our presence. I tried hard not to shudder as I led my friends down the passageway to the back door. The body was long gone. There was nothing to be afraid of.

The door was still unlocked. Poor Evelyn; she'd be mortified if she ever knew she'd left it that way. I'd have to make sure it was secure when we left.

We'd all brought flashlights; I was risking no lights this time, not even in Spragge's office. We'd decided to start there, as the most likely spot.

"What we need is something, anything, that would serve as proof," I pontificated. "The ideal thing would be some of Monahan's identification. His body is certainly in the river, but I'm not sure I would have thrown him in, passport and all, if I'd been Fortier. Bodies surface eventually, and passports are printed on good sturdy paper that could still be read, I'll bet."

"I'd burn his papers, myself," said Nigel skeptically.

"So would I, and they probably did just that, but there's a chance they forgot something," I insisted. "Then there are Monahan's clothes, his luggage."

"Also in the river." Nigel was determined to look on the dark side.

"Maybe. Look, there has to be *something*. Maybe we can find the poison they used."

"Poison?" Three pairs of eyes stared at me.

"Well, it must have been, don't you think?" I was surprised I had to explain; it seemed so obvious. "He wouldn't just die like that, quietly and with no fuss, any other way. Someone, probably the 'doctor,' got on the train and managed to slip poison into Bill's coffee, probably when he picked it up at the buffet window. It would be easy enough on a moving train. I admit the odds are against our finding it. I think the best way is just to look for anything at all that seems out of the ordinary. And for goodness' sakes keep your ears open, in case Fortier decides to finish his cleanup job tonight."

We were quiet, and thorough, but there was nothing. We combed Spragge's office. Unlike Fortier's domain, it was very tidy and easy to search. Even the laptop computer that might have yielded a few more secrets was gone.

Tom went methodically through Spragge's paper files, searching for irregular business practices. Nigel closed the velvet draperies, turned on the desktop computer, and went through its files with equal doggedness and equal results: zero. Lynn and I, with no particular expertise, simply looked through everything else, hunting with a woman's eye for personal details that didn't seem to fit.

In an hour we called it quits for that office and

moved on to Fortier's. It would be tedious to detail that search. His files were still there, which was encouraging, but otherwise our exploration was fruitless. So were the searches through the other offices, which yielded exactly no information at all, except that Brian Upton had emptied his desk of the illegal drugs.

"Heard about the police being here, I expect," said Lynn. "It's a good thing he got here before we did." She yawned, not really very interested in what she was saying. None of us was much interested in much of anything by then.

We had repaired to my cubbyhole. I sat down at my desk with a groan. "We might as well give up. It isn't here, whatever it is, or at least we can't find it. And Shepherd will get here tomorrow and unleash the police, and goodness only knows what will happen. Let's go home, Tom. Sufficient unto the day."

I put hand on the corner of my desk to help heave myself out of my chair, and knocked off the book that Evelyn had lent me. Nigel stooped to pick it up.

"Oh, sorry, your bookmark fell out, Dorothy."

"What bookmark? I wasn't reading it. Let me see."

And there it was, what four of us had been seeking for hours. I leaned against the desk and indulged in near-hysterics while the others waited, dumbfounded. When I recovered, I shone my flashlight on the "bookmark" and held it out in an unsteady hand for the others to see.

It was a small piece of card stock, about two by

three inches. Computer-generated, it had several lines of type in an undecipherable code, but the rest was plain enough.

"SFO LGW BA 800 03JUN," it read. And below that, "LGW SFO BA 801 21JUN."

"What is it?" said Nigel, puzzled.

"My God!" breathed Tom.

"It's the stub of a boarding pass," I said in a shaky voice. "A flight from San Francisco to London Gatwick, British Airways flight 800 on June 3. The return flight is shown, too. He'd planned to go home today." My voice broke.

"Who planned? I don't understand." Lynn's voice was plaintive.

I held the flashlight higher, so they could read the top line.

"MONAHAN/WILLIAM."

TWENTY

"BUT—WHAT'S Bill Monahan's boarding pass doing in your book?"

"That," I said, beginning to catch a glimmer of the truth, "is not my book."

"It was on your desk—"

"I borrowed it. Or rather, I had it thrust upon me. And I have been an idiot."

This time they didn't ask, but simply waited for me to gather my thoughts.

"That book," I said when I had put it together in my head, "was loaned to me by Evelyn Forbes. It was in her bottom file drawer, with a couple of other paperbacks. It isn't quite her style, though. She prefers Golden Age mysteries or classic thrillers, John Buchan for choice.

"Therefore, I believe that she didn't buy that book. It doesn't look new, anyway. And in fact it isn't new. I've seen it myself, a couple of weeks ago. It belonged to Monahan. He was reading it on the train until he started talking to me, and I saw it on the seat next to him. And if I hadn't been, as I said, a total nincompoop, I would have remembered before now. He probably bought it to read on the plane on the way over. That would explain the boarding pass. They're handy bookmarks; I've used them myself."

"So what was it doing in Forbes's office?" Lynn made an excellent straight man.

"That's the sixty-four-dollar question, isn't it? But the answer is obvious. Somebody involved in Monahan's murder saw it with the poor man's things and didn't have the heart to throw it out. And I think I know who."

"Okay, I'll bite." Tom this time.

I told them.

When I'd finished explaining, Lynn groaned. "And you *still* have no proof."

"No. But now I know how to get it. Or at least I intend to have a very good shot at it. Let's get out of here now, before somebody catches us, and we can brainstorm on the way home."

They were a big help, all three of them. Nigel spent hours on Tom's computer, checking airline bookings, while Tom spent hours on the phone with the Home Office, pulling strings. By morning we were primed and ready to go.

"Good luck, Dorothy!" Lynn gave me a hug and a kiss. Tom and Nigel were already off about their own business.

"I'm going to need it, but if things work out at all according to plan, I should be all right. Are you sure you—"

"No, I'll be waiting right here, with bated breath."

English weather is a study in rapid contrast. Last night had been overcast, with the threat of imminent rain. Today was right out of the tourist brochures, bright and warm, the first day of summer. Another time I might have walked all the way to the office. It was less than three miles by foot, and walking in London on a gorgeous day is one of my very favorite occupations. This time, though, I hurried off to Belgrave Square, the nearest place to find a taxi. I needed all my energy today.

Evelyn was just going up the steps as I arrived. She looked about a hundred years old. Her shoulders were bowed, her hair in disarray. I was careful not to be too ebullient with my greeting; she looked as though anything approaching enthusiasm would be unwelcome.

"Good morning, Mrs. Forbes."

"Oh. Good morning, Mrs. Wren." She turned and went into her own office without another word. I didn't push it. She'd have enough harassment later.

Mr. Spragge was in already, having arrived even before the punctual Mrs. Forbes. Mr. Grey followed us by a few minutes, looking nondescript; then Mr. Hammond, looking hungover, and Mr. Upton, looking even worse-tempered than usual. I paid very little attention to any of them. I had worries of my own.

Timing was everything this morning. There were two variables over which I had no control, and I was nervous about them. The first was the British Airways schedule. If the plane was late, it might yet spoil everything—but there was no point in worrying about that, I told myself. Planes are either on time or else they're not, and fretting won't make them land one second sooner.

The second was Mr. Fortier. He might not come in

at all, but I thought he would. He wasn't stupid; he knew things were coming to a head. No, he'd come, and he'd leave just as soon as he could, and there I thought I might be able to exercise a little gentle persuasion, though at some personal risk.

He walked in the door at about ten, looking extremely annoyed and almost furtive. I was mightily relieved to see him.

"Mr. Fortier, I don't believe we've formally met," I said sweetly, rising from my desk and extending my hand. "I'm Louise Wren, the new receptionist. You were here the other day, but very much occupied with Mr. Spragge; we had no chance to talk. I'm very glad to meet you."

He shook my hand, since he couldn't very well get out of it, but without any marked enthusiasm, and turned to go to his office.

"I understand you're Canadian. I, as you can tell, am an expat American. I've always enjoyed Canada; my late husband and I used to visit Nova Scotia, and we loved it. What part of Canada do you come from?"

"British Columbia."

"Oh, my, right the other side of the country. Vancouver?"

"Yes."

"I've always wanted to go there. I love our own Pacific Northwest. Is Vancouver anything like Seattle?"

"I don't know. Excuse me."

So much for gentle persuasion. That little effort at

delaying techniques had taken up a minute at most. I looked at my watch. If the plane was on time, it had been on the ground for almost two hours. Within the next half hour, surely?

Five minutes later Vicki Shore and Lloyd Pierce walked in, looking unnaturally solemn. I nodded gravely to them; they said nothing, but walked on into their office.

I sat at my desk, answering the telephone, staving off reporters, watching the clock.

The door from the main office opened. Mr. Fortier walked past me, his arms full of papers.

I jumped up as though bitten. "Oh, let me help you with those," I cried, and managed to bump into him. The papers cascaded to the floor.

Mr. Hammond, who had just popped out of the main office, was right behind me. He had a cigarette in his hand; somehow ash got spilled on a file folder, and when Mr. Hammond bent down to brush it off, his cigarette fell on another file.

"Oh, dear, that might start a fire!" I grabbed a half-empty cup of cold tea from my desk and poured it over cigarette and file folder. Looking at what I'd done, I put my hand to my mouth and picked up the ruined folder. "Oh, Mr. Fortier, I'm so sorry! I'm afraid I haven't done your file a bit of good."

Fortier was not at all amused. "*Thank* you, Mrs.—er—I believe I can do nicely *without* your help! If you'll kindly step aside—"

The front door opened. Tom Anderson stepped inside, with a tall, lanky man behind him. I breathed a heartfelt sigh of relief and dropped both the file and my ditsy persona.

"Good," I said crisply, nodding to the tall man, whose strong jaw was grimly set. "Mr. Fortier, I forgot to mention that Mr. Spragge would like to speak to you for a moment. If you would come this way, please?"

I thought he was going to bolt, but Tom and the tall man filled the doorway. With a scowl and a shrug, Fortier walked back into Evelyn's office. I followed him, everyone else trailing after me.

"Evelyn, we need Mr. Spragge, please. This gentleman"—I indicated the tall man—"wishes to speak to him, quite urgently."

This was the really tricky part. Evelyn was under no obligation to obey orders from me, of all people. But I put steel into my voice, the kind that any elementary school teacher knows how to use when necessary, and she picked up the phone and spoke into it. Mr. Spragge's door opened, and he came out, and Tom put his fingers to his mouth and uttered a piercing whistle.

That brought everyone else out of their cubbyholes—Grey, Upton, Shore, Pierce. It was really rather crowded in the main office, and when, on his cue, Nigel walked in with Sneaky Pete in his arms, there was a small sensation. The cat ignored the crowd, came straight up to me, stropped itself against my ankles, and started to purr.

"That cat again!" said Evelyn. "Mrs. Wren, what is the meaning of—I know that cat," she said, her voice suddenly rising. "He's the one—oh! So it was *you* that night—"

"It was," I said calmly. "Yes, I thought you would recognize poor old Pete eventually, though he's a good deal handsomer than when you first saw him. But I think you might be more interested in this gentleman. He's from America—from Multilinks, in fact. May I present Mr. Bill Monahan?"

Everyone was startled. Three mouths dropped open; fear entered three pairs of eyes. But only one scream sounded.

"No! No, he can't be! No, he doesn't look like that at all, and I put him in the river myself! No, it isn't—make him go away!"

In the end it took two police constables to subdue Evelyn Forbes.

TWENTY-ONE

"SHE WAS ON THE verge of a breakdown, anyway," I said later as I sipped good bourbon and relaxed in Lynn's living room. Walt Shepherd was closeted with the police. Messrs. Spragge and Fortier and Mrs. Forbes were cooling their heels at Her Majesty's pleasure. The rest of the Multilinks staff were, presumably, out looking for jobs, except for Mr. Hammond, who was sitting with the Andersons and Nigel and me, tying up loose ends.

"I almost hated to do it to her," I went on. "She was in many ways a very nice woman."

"Nice!" Lynn gave a dramatic little shudder. "She killed two people!"

"Only one, strictly speaking, poor little Mr. Dalal. It was Fortier's hand that administered the poison to Monahan, though I'm pretty sure Evelyn brewed it."

"Brewed it? What do you mean?" Lynn was eager for all the details.

"I think she boiled it up herself. They obviously can't do an autopsy when they haven't got a body, but if it ever turns up, I'm betting they find nicotine."

Terry looked at his just-lit cigarette and very casually stubbed it out.

"I know a little about poisons," I said modestly. "Anybody who's read as many mysteries as I have learns something over the years about how to kill people. Nicotine is about the only thing I can think of that fits the way Monahan died. He was perfectly all right, and then half an hour later he was dead—with a cup of coffee in front of him. Now, nicotine has a strong taste, but the coffee on English trains is bad enough to hide the taste of almost anything. Nicotine is also extremely lethal in very small doses, and even less if a person doesn't smoke. And nicotine works extremely fast. If poor Bill had any kind of ulcer in his mouth or a cut on his lip, it would have started to kill him even faster than usual. Finally, nicotine is one of the easiest poisons to make at home. And no, I have no intention of telling you how. One of you might get ideas someday.''

''It's guesswork,'' objected Tom lazily.

''Not entirely. One of the books in Evelyn's file drawer was a Dorothy Sayers, *Hangman's Holiday*. I've read it many times. It's a collection of short stories, one of which features nicotine as an efficient poison. And of course Evelyn may admit it.''

''What about Dalal? I suppose he stumbled onto something?'' Terry sipped the scotch I'd had Lynn load with soda.

''I think she killed Dalal for the same reason she arranged Monahan's death: He suspected something was wrong at Multilinks. You see, it all stems from her hero worship of Mr. Spragge. He was the great man, the god, the one who could do no wrong. So, of course, when he—with Fortier's collaboration, we've established that now from the computer records—when they started pirating their own software and selling it to the third-world nations at a deep discount, and Evelyn found out about it, Spragge of course had to be protected at all costs.''

"But why did he do it?" Terry asked in exasperation. "That's the part I find absolutely incredible."

"I'm not sure even he knows that. He may have done it, or persuaded himself he was doing it, from humanitarian motives. I heard him tell one of the policemen that he knew a lot of his customers from way back, Oxford days. But eventually he fell prey to the lure of the money. His wife's an invalid, you know, and specialized medical care costs a lot of money, even in this country. I think he was going to get out, though. Fortier I'm not so sure about. He says he was, but he showed every sign of skipping the country. You helped prevent that, Terry, and I'm so glad you agreed to cooperate.''

There was a long pause, then Lynn sighed. "That poor woman.''

"Yes," I agreed sadly. "You know, if I'd been as smart as I sometimes think I am, I'd have guessed much earlier, just from her reading material. She loved John Buchan. I think she imagined herself a kind of Richard Hannay, brave and alone, fighting for Civilization As We Know It.''

We were all quiet then, until the silence was shattered by a strident feline demand. Pete had finished his supper—plebeian tuna fish this time, but laced with caviar—and wanted some attention. He strolled over and arched his back, demanding a caress, and when I stroked his back, collapsed onto the floor and rolled over so that I could pet his tummy.

I obliged, and then stroked it more purposefully to the accompaniment of loud purrs. I looked up at Nigel.

"Um, Nigel," I said, making a little face, "you and Inga are definitely adopting this cat, yes?"

"Right. He's a friendly little bloke, now that he's got used to us, and getting more handsome by the minute as he puts on weight. Anyway, he helped unmask a murderer; he's a very exceptional cat. Why?"

"Only that I hope you have some good friends who are as yet catless. Because he is a she, and she's going to have kittens." I poked gently at the wiggly little lumps under Pete's belly fur. Nigel picked up the cat and felt for himself, and his face was a study in consternation.

The doorbell rang. Lynn sat up with a groan. "Who on earth?"

"The police, I suppose," said Tom, sighing and getting to his feet. "They said they might still have some questions, although I thought they meant tomorrow. I'll go."

In a moment there was a basso rumble from the downstairs hall. I pricked up my ears unbelievingly, then scrambled from my deep chair and ran like a teenager down the stairs, my arms spread wide.

"Alan!"

Marlys Millhiser

NOBODY DIES IN A casino

A CHARLIE GREENE MYSTERY

Where does a Los Angeles literary agent go for some rest and relaxation? Feeling lucky, Charlie Greene gambles on Las Vegas, never anticipating the stakes will be murder. Make that seven murders. In seven days.

It begins with the hit-and-run death, which Charlie has the bad luck to witness. Then the cop she tells her story to has a fatal "accident." Toss in a hot new client with an avid interest in the government's top-secret "Area 51," a casino robbery and $200,000 in missing cash—and it all adds up to more trouble than Charlie can handle.

Available January 2001 at your favorite retail outlet.

A SAM McCALL MYSTERY

Eric C. Evans

ENDANGERED

A savvy campaign manager is always prepared to
expect the worst during a heated political race. But
Sam McCall never anticipated murder.

He's worked for Utah state senator Maggie Hansen for
fifteen years. Now, in her bid for one last term in
office, a sensational murder rocks the campaign. The
chief suspect is the senator's brother.

Sam's primary objective is to get to the truth. With
the press turning up the heat and the opposition
having a field day, he's running out of time. But he
knows that in politics the best defense is a good
offense. Unfortunately, so does a killer.

Available January 2001 at your favorite retail outlet.

WORLDWIDE LIBRARY®

WEE373